The
Rage

MICHAEL CHAMBERS

ISBN: 9798636083740

DEDICATION

For the survivors.

Never stop fighting.

If you are struggling with thoughts of suicide,
please don't give up. The world needs you here.

National Suicide Prevention Lifeline

1-800-273-8255

CONTENTS

ACKNOWLEDGMENTS

I'd like to thank the

MISSOURI POLICE CHIEF'S ASSOCIATION

and the

AMERICAN FOUNDATION FOR SUICIDE PREVENTION

for their invaluable assistance. Any errors in procedure or information are solely my responsibility.

CHAPTER ONE

"Hey, you coming tonight?" Laurel said as Soo Jung stood at her locker, putting away her books. "I hear Chase is coming."

"I'll be there," Soo Jung said, smiling despite herself. "It's gonna be awesome."

"I know," Laurel said. She looked around to make sure no one was listening as she spoke quietly. "So, you gonna finally quit hiding and make your move?"

"I'm not hiding," Soo Jung said, but Laurel just shook her head.

"No, of course not. That's why you run away every time you see him," she said. "I talked to Clint this morning, and he says Chase won't shut up about you."

"You didn't," Soo Jung said, and Laurel smiled.

"You won't go get him, I'll just have to step in and make it happen," she said. "Seriously, he's totally hot, has an actual brain, and is completely into you. What's the problem?"

"I don't know," Soo Jung said. "Every time I try to talk

to him, I turn into some kind of babbling idiot. Lots of 'ers' and 'ums,' and I'm scared to death I'll snort or drool or something."

Laurel laughed as they walked down the hall. They stopped outside the gym. "Look, you just gotta relax a little. Let his yellow fever sink in, and he's all yours."

"Racist," Soo Jung said, and Laurel laughed.

"Snowflake," she said, and soon they were both laughing. "Look, I gotta get to practice. You want to meet up before we go?"

"Yeah," Soo Jung said. "You can help me pick out an outfit."

****

Dana sat on the hood of her patrol car outside the high school, watching as kids piled into farm trucks and beater cars that barely passed inspections and drove off the school parking lot. She was parked right next to the exit, nice and visible to deter the worst of the stupidity. It was a boring post, like most of them, but a necessary one.

"One oh one to one hundred," her radio crackled, and she smiled.

"It's just the two of us, Mark," she said into the radio. "Pretty sure we don't need service numbers."

"Copy that," Mark said. He was a good man, a natural cop, but Lord he loved protocols. It had taken three months after she'd hired him to get him to understand they didn't use ten codes. "Chief, you might want to join me out here at the bowling alley. Looks like there might be a spot of trouble."

"Lord help me," she said, shaking her head. "What's the problem, Mark?" she said into the microphone.

"Jason Hill's got himself a pretty good head of steam going again," Mark said, and Dana shook her head. "He listens to you better."

"Chief Atwater to dispatch," she said into the mic.

"Go ahead, Chief," Earl said. Earl was her only dispatcher, a generally cranky old fart who'd been the Chief until he'd retired last year, and they'd hired her to take his place. An inveterate grouch, Earl could usually be counted on to keep the bullshit to a minimum.

"Wendall on yet?" she said.

"Just signed on," Earl said, sounding annoyed. It was just now three fifteen; Wendall's shift started at three, which meant he'd be ready to go by three twenty or so. She was a little surprised he was ready to go this early. "You want me to send him out to you?"

"No," she said, making the decision. Mark was a first-rate officer, but he could stand to be a little more assertive. Time to get his feet wet, she decided. "Send him over to give Mark a hand."

"Copy that," Earl said. "You catch that, kid?" he said over the radio, and Dana cringed.

"Ten-four, Sir," Mark said, sounding mildly annoyed as Dana shook her head. "How do you want us to proceed, Chief?"

"If he's out of line, bring him in," she said firmly. "Wendall will back you up."

"Copy that," Mark said.

"I'm three minutes out," Wendall said over the radio.

"Copy that," Mark said. Dana shook her head again and went back to glaring at students as they drove off. Satisfied she'd at least put a crimp in the hijinks for the afternoon, she climbed back in behind the wheel and drove off, taking one more lap around town before heading back to the station to try and tackle the small mountain of paperwork that was no doubt waiting for her.

****

"Afternoon," Earl said as she came through the door. "Just made a fresh pot of coffee, if you're interested."

"Sounds great," she said. He stood up, and she held up her hand. "Earl, you are not my assistant. You're a dispatcher."

"I made anyone in earshot grab my coffee when I wore that badge," he said with a smile. "It's expected."

"Not by me," she said, smiling and shaking her head as

13

she poured a cup of coffee. "Any messages?"

"That idiot Mayor Shelby called, wanted to remind you that he'll need the parade route blocked off for this weekend. I told him we haven't forgotten the damned thing in twenty years, not likely to start now."

"I hope you put it a little nicer than that," she said, laughing.

"Miss Macy called for you," he said. "Said she'd try you at home later." She felt a brief moment of panic when Earl mentioned her name, but she made herself calm down. Earl was a crusty old bastard, but he kept himself out of other people's business. She didn't doubt for a minute he knew all about her and Macy, but he didn't judge.

"Heard anything from Mark or Wendall?" she said, hoping to change the subject, purely for her own comfort.

"Not yet," he said.

"Been a while," she said, looking at the clock on the wall; it was a quarter to four. "Maybe I should go check on them."

"Kid's gonna have to grow a set sooner or later," Earl said, shrugging. "He can't handle one old drunk, might be time to look for a different job."

He might be coarser than sandpaper, and generally unpleasant if you didn't know to ignore his grouching, but Earl knew the job. As much as she wanted to look out for her deputies, he was right. If they couldn't handle a drunk, then they had no business on the job. She'd carried Mark long enough.

"I'll be in my office, going paper blind," she said, and he laughed.

"You know, any time I start to think I might miss the job, all I have to do is remember the paperwork, and I'm happy," he said, and she laughed with him.

"That's why they pay me the big bucks, right?" she said.

"Tell you what," he said. "We don't hear from them in five minutes or so, I'll swing by on my way home and check on them."

"You don't have to do that," she said, but he shook his head.

"I'm old, not dead," he said. "Day I can't handle one drunken jackass is the day I actually do retire."

"Just try not to hurt anyone," she said. "And do me a favor? Go easy on him, at least over the radio."

"Yes ma'am," Earl said, nodding.

She was headed for her office when the front door opened. Mark and Wendall came through the door, looking like Mutt and Jeff after a tour of hell. Where Mark was short and a little on the lanky side, Wendall was tall and wide, with no discernible neck and arms the size of tree trunks. Both were dirty and disheveled. Mark's uniform shirt was torn, and there was a large hole in Wendall's pant leg.

They were dragging a large, angry man inside in handcuffs, yelling and struggling the whole time as they took him to the only cell, which was nothing more than a cage in the far corner.

"I said get the fuck off me," Jason Hill said, trying to jerk his arms free. Mark snaked an arm between his, grabbing him by the shoulder and levering him down as Wendall bent his wrist.

"Shut up," Mark said as Earl stood up and grabbed the keys to the cell, opening the door for them.

"The fuck you looking at, old man?" Jason said as Earl stood by the open door.

"A loud-mouthed little butt squirt that's gonna be shitting teeth for a week if he don't shut up and sit down," Earl said, staring him down. Earl might have been getting old, but he hadn't lost a bit of his edge. Hill shut up and stood still as Wendall uncuffed him and moved him away from the cell door.

"I take it everything went okay?" Dana said, looking them over as she tried not to laugh. They looked like hell, and judging by the look on Wendall's face, they weren't feeling much better.

"My best freaking pants," he said, looking at the tear in his pant leg.

"Not any more," she said, still trying not to laugh. She let them get back to work; Mark started to fill out the incident report as Wendall went into the bathroom to change into a clean uniform. She turned her attention to the cell, where Hill was pacing back and forth.

"What happened this time, Jason?" she said. "Shirley cut you off again?"

"I wasn't bothering nobody," he said, and she caught a whiff of him. He smelled like cheap whiskey, and she knew he'd been drinking before he got to the bowling alley; under city ordinance, they were only licensed to serve beer, not hard liquor. "Look, cut me loose, and I'll go home."

"After you sober up," she said, and he growled, slamming his hands into the bars. Earl stood up, but she shook her head slightly as Hill continued to throw his fit.

"Shut up and sit down," she said firmly, and he went back to pacing. "I said sit down," she said again, and he did as he was told, giving her the stink-eye.

"I'll go right home and stay there," he said. "I miss work again, and I'm gonna get fired."

"You're not going anywhere tonight," she said. "You sober up and manage not to show your ass any more tonight, and I'll make sure you're out in time for work. Fair enough?"

It seemed to pacify him, because he relaxed and laid down on the cot. She'd bet money she didn't have he'd be dead to the world in thirty minutes. She walked past Earl's desk on her way to the office.

"He acts up again, let someone know," she said.

"I can handle him," Earl said, and she shook her head.

"Probably," she said, "but you throw your back out again, and I'm up a creek. Let Wendall deal with him, okay?"

"Yes ma'am," he said, looking less than thrilled. She patted him on the shoulder and went to tackle the papers waiting for her.

CHAPTER TWO

"That's the one," Laurel said as Soo Jung held up a bright green blouse. "And those jeans."

"They're so tight," Soo Jung said, looking at the jeans in her hand.

"Exactly," Laurel said. "You have this amazing short-girl ass. He won't be able to stop staring." They chattered almost non-stop as she dressed, excited. This party had been weeks in the making, and everyone was going. Well, everyone who mattered, anyway. Most of the senior class would be there.

"Did you hear who Roy Cole is bringing?" Laurel said. "Janelle Stuart."

"Not exactly a surprise," Soo Jung said. "They've been screwing like bunnies all year."

"Yeah, but she's a sophomore," Laurel said. "I thought this was supposed to be a seniors thing."

"Well, Roy's a senior," she said, shrugging as she checked herself out in the mirror. "I should get a boob job."

"Oh, please," Laurel said. "You look great."

"I'm barely an A cup," she said. "I swear, I'm built like a ten year old boy."

"You're crazy," Laurel said. "Besides, Chase is an ass man."

Soo Jung threw a pillow at her as they laughed. "Tell that to Heidi Galloway," she said.

"Handjob Heidi?" Laurel said, shaking her head. "Trust me, you won't be so jealous when you see her in twenty years and those knockers of hers have to be tied together so she doesn't trip on them."

Soo Jung shrugged and picked up two pairs of shoes. "Heels or flats?" she said.

"Flats," Laurel said. "We'll be in the woods, remember? Besides, you're tiny and adorable. Use it. Guys like short chicks."

"Again, tell that to Heidi," she said, and Laurel rolled her eyes.

"You've got a serious complex over that bitch," Laurel said. "You've got to stop comparing yourself to her. She's just another cornfed farm girl. You're the token Asian chick in town, all tiny and exotic. Now, put on your best delicate look, and let's go see if we can't turn some heads."

****

Laurel parked her car next to the others. It was a short walk down the path to the clearing where the party was being held. They could already hear music thumping and people laughing.

"How late are we?" Soo Jung said.

"Just late enough," Laurel said. "Why do you think we stopped for ice cream on the way?"

"In the vain hope I'll someday have hips?" Soo Jung said, and Laurel laughed.

"So we can make a proper entrance," Laurel said. "Come on, I want to see everyone's jaws drop when you walk in."

"Like that's going to happen," she said, but Laurel dragged her down the path to the party. Her breath caught for a moment when she saw Chase standing by the stereo, a red plastic cup in one hand as he talked to a tall, voluptuous blonde.

"Oh crap," Soo Jung said, stopping short. "She's already on him."

"Not for long," Laurel said, smiling. "Now come on." They walked into the clearing, stopping just long enough to get drinks from the coolers before Laurel practically shoved her toward Chase.

"Hey," he said, all smiles as he turned to her. "Glad you could make it."

"So am I," Soo Jung said.

"You look great," he said, unable to stop staring. Heidi cleared her throat, and Soo Jung found herself smiling as Laurel slipped up behind them.

"Hey, Heidi," Laurel said. "I love that top. Where'd you get it?" She led Heidi away, looking like she'd just bitten into a lemon as they left the two of them standing together.

"Hope I wasn't interrupting anything," Soo Jung said, and he shook his head, sandy blonde hair falling across his face as he smiled.

"Not at all," he said. "So, you wanna see it?"

"See what?" she said, caught somewhere between embarrassed and excited.

"Come on," he said, smiling as the group began to break up, wandering further into the woods in twos and threes. She saw Laurel walking with Clint, hand in his and laughing at something he'd just said. Roy and Janelle walked past them as Chase held out his hand.

She took his hand and walked with him, aware of how small she was compared to him. At four foot ten, she was almost a foot and a half shorter than he was, and she was reasonably certain he could carry her around in one hand. His broad linebacker shoulders seemed impossible large next to her tiny frame, and her small hand was almost lost in his as they walked.

"So, is it big?" she asked, and it was his turn to blush. "I mean, it'd have to be for all of us, right?"

"You're doing that on purpose," he said, grinning.

"Maybe," she said, smiling. What the hell, she thought. Maybe Laurel was right; it was time to use what she had instead of worrying about what she didn't have. She put her arms around one of his massive ones as they walked.

"You really do look great," he said, and she was surprised to see how nervous he was. Before she could talk herself out of it, she pulled him down and gave him a kiss.

"Been wanting to do that for a long time," she said, staring up at him. He looked like she'd just clobbered him with a clown hammer, and she smiled as they walked further into the woods. She walked slowly, enjoying the hard feel of him against her, and by the time they made it to the second clearing further into the woods, everyone else was already there.

She walked with him up the long flight of steps to the giant wooden platform, taking one of the last open spots next to him. It was built in a large circle, with an opening in the center where a small fire had been set up. Chase bent down and whispered in her ear as he pulled a Zippo from his pocket and flipped it open.

"I'm really glad you're here with me," he said. "You look beautiful."

She was a little annoyed at herself as she blushed, but she forgot all about it when he kissed her. She was dimly aware that they weren't the only ones kissing. She saw Lauren and Clint making out, and Roy and Janelle were oblivious to the rest of them on the other side of Chase. Those who weren't making out were holding hands and smiling at each other. Even Heidi, who she'd been convinced didn't know what nice was, smiled as she complimented another girl's hair, and they hugged.

Chase stood up, still holding her hand with his left as he struck the lighter in his right. "Let's get this party started," he said loudly, and everyone clapped and cheered as he tossed the lighter into the wood pile, and the fire roared to life.

Soo Jung watched as everyone slipped the necklaces over their heads, and did the same. Someone had remembered to get one the right size for her, and she was betting it was

Chase.

"Class of 2019," Chase said loudly, and everyone cheered again. "Are you ready?"

More cheering and clapping answered him, and she squeezed his hand, still blown away she was with him when so many other girls would have done anything to be in her place. He bent down and kissed her cheek. "You want to do the countdown?" he whispered, and she smiled.

"Sure," she said, beaming as all eyes turned to her. "Ready? Five," she said, smiling uncontrollably. Laurel gave her a wink and a nod, and she nodded back.

"Four," she said, surprised to see that Heidi was smiling at her as well. She'd been after Chase all year, and wasn't known for losing gracefully. But the look on her face as Soo Jung counted down could only be described as admiration, and she even blew Soo Jung a kiss as she smiled.

"Three," she said. All around her were her the classmates who'd quickly become friends. Her family had only moved here a year ago, but she couldn't imagine living anywhere else.

"Two," she called out, excitement building as everyone watched her. She could feel their eyes on her, and everyone was smiling and happy as they waited for her to give the word. This was going to be the best party ever.

"One," she said, smiling as Chase kissed her hand, and they all jumped together. Twenty nooses slammed tight as bodies dropped fifteen feet, coming to an abrupt stop a foot above the ground as the sharp jerk and the impact of the heavy knots snapped their spines.

****

Dana parked the cruiser in the driveway, taking a moment to make sure the shotgun in the rack was locked up tight and all the electronics were shut down before she got out and walked up the sidewalk, letting herself in the front door.

"You're back," Macy said as she came in and went straight to the closet, putting her gun away and hanging her duty belt up. "Figured you'd be later."

"Slow day," she said as Macy came to her. She kissed her, lightly at first, but Dana found herself responding as Macy pulled back.

"Down, tiger," she said, patting her cheek. "Dinner will be ready soon."

"You didn't have to cook," Dana said.

"I don't mind," she said. "Besides, tell me you wouldn't have ended up just grabbing a burger if I hadn't. Go on, I dare you."

"Probably," Dana said, smiling as she followed her into the kitchen, enjoying the way her hips moved as she walked. She'd worn Dana's favorite jeans, the ones that showed off her ass so well, and a brilliant blue tank top that did little to hide the rest of her. Her dark hair, long in a way Dana could only envy, hung down to the middle of her back in a fall of loose curls. Her own rather limp blonde locks were tied back in a severe ponytail to keep it out of the way, and she let it down as Macy set a plate in front of her and poured the wine.

She waited patiently as Macy said grace. It never ceased to amaze her how much faith Macy had, especially considering how so many so-called Christians felt about their lifestyle.

"God doesn't hate," Macy would say every time she asked. "He just loves us all. Hate is a human thing."

"So, slow day, huh?" Macy said, and Dana nodded.

"One arrest, and I wasn't even in on it," she said. "I tell you, it's like I moved to a small, peaceful town or something."

"Heaven forbid," Macy said with a smile. "You'd think someone could start a crime wave, just out of courtesy."

"Don't tease," Dana said, smiling. "I'm not sure I could take that much excitement. And how goes the fight for you?"

"Stamping out ignorance, one student at a time," she said, smiling. Macy was something of a town fixture; the only openly gay teacher in town, the hostility one expected from small town people was mollified somewhat by her devout religious beliefs. "The animals are having a big senior party tonight, which of course they've convinced themselves they've managed to keep a total secret."

"Fun times," Dana said, and Macy smiled. "Be a few of them dragging ass tomorrow."

"I'll be sure to talk extra loud," she said, and Dana laughed. She'd done her fair share of drinking in high school, and she was convinced that the teachers not only knew, they made sure to be as loud as possible the next day just to torture her.

"Well, let's hope they at least behave themselves enough to stay out of trouble," she said. "Because I really, really don't want to go back into work tonight."

"I was hoping you'd say that," she said, refilling her wine glass. "I was planning on getting you drunk and taking advantage of you later."

"Diabolical," Dana said, smiling over her wine glass.

CHAPTER THREE

Dana lay in bed, listening to the slow, steady rhythm of Macy's breathing as she slept with one arm over her. She knew she should get some sleep; five thirty came disturbingly early in the morning, and she would have her hands full, getting ready for the parade this weekend. For now, she was content to lie there and feel the soft woman lying against her, enveloped in the warm smell of vanilla and coconut from her hair.

She knew none of it was fair to Macy; the coded telephone messages, parking her car in back of the house so it wouldn't be seen from the street, the sneaking around and never going out. It wasn't Macy's fault she wasn't out, and she deserved better. She deserved to go on a real date, instead of hiding in Dana's house.

She kissed the top of her head as she stirred. "Trouble sleeping?" Macy said, and Dana nodded.

"Usually," she said, stroking her hair. "You should get some rest."

Macy kissed her, one hand trailing across her stomach. "Put me to sleep," she said with a smile.

Dana pushed her back onto the bed and hovered over her for a minute, just enjoying the sight of her. She bent down and kissed her neck lightly, and Macy gasped as she melted into the pillow. Her own body was beginning to respond when her phone rang on the nightstand, and they both groaned. Macy let out a disappointed laugh.

"I swear, I'm handing out pop quizzes first thing in the morning," she said, and Dana smiled as she picked up the phone. It was Wendall, of course. The alarm clock said it was just after one in the morning.

"Atwater," she said, answering it. She fought the urge to giggle as Macy tickled her bare ass, and she slapped at her hand as Macy smiled, then started kissing her shoulder blades. A shiver went down her spine, and she almost moaned into the phone. "What's up, Wendall?"

"Sorry to call you in the middle of the night, Chief, but I think we might have a situation here," he said. He might be chronically allergic to punctuality, and his reports read like he'd written them in pig Latin, but Wendall was a solid cop, and he didn't call her over a maybe.

"I'm awake anyway," she said as Macy kissed her bare hip, and her eyes rolled back in her head as she tried to keep it together. "What's up?"

"Phones are ringing off the hook," he said. "Must have taken twenty calls in the last hour, all of them from parents whose kids haven't come home yet."

"There's supposed to be a senior class party tonight," she said. "Probably all out drunk in the woods."

"Kind of what I figured," he said. "So I swung by all the popular spots. Found a lot of cars parked out by Hanger's Woods, but no one around. Music still playing, lots of beer on ice."

"Like I said, a party," she said. "I'll meet you out there, and we'll see if we can't break it up. Give me fifteen minutes," she said, and she almost gasped as Macy nibbled on her shoulder.

"Better make that thirty minutes," she said.

"I'll get started," he said, and she could have sworn he sounded like he was laughing. She hung up as Macy pulled her back onto the bed.

"I've got to go to work," she said, and Macy smiled.

"Then stop wasting time," she said with a wicked grin.

****

She pulled into the open space near Hanger's Woods, next to Wendall's patrol car. "Plates match some of the reported missing," he said.

"Well, let's go take a look," she said, trying not to sound too annoyed. "Weren't you supposed to be off shift a couple of hours ago?"

"Travis has court in the morning on that pot bust last month," he said. "Told him I'd take his shift so he didn't walk into court and get accidentally shot for a zombie. We filled out the shift change papers."

"Probably just buried under the rest of it," she admitted. She was woefully behind on that end of the job. Given how slow things had been lately, she really had no excuse; she was just procrastinating because she hated paperwork.

They walked into the clearing. As he'd said, there was a radio still playing some obnoxious pop song, and there were several coolers still full of ice water and cheap beer. "You see what I see?" Wendall said, and she nodded.

"Unless they brought enough beer for the whole fleet, I don't think much drinking happened out here tonight." She looked around, and noticed something else. "No empties."

"Trash can by the stereo," Wendall said. "Barely a sixer's worth in it."

"Lightweights," Dana said, and Wendall chuckled. "You grew up around here. Where would they go that's close enough to walk?"

"There's another clearing maybe a half-mile in," he said, pointing deeper into the woods. "Little bigger than this. We never partied in this one; too easy for cops like us to drive right up and catch us."

"Lazy lightweights," she said, and he laughed again.

26

"Well, I suppose we should break it up, don't you?"

"Spank 'em all and send 'em home to Mommy?" he said, and she nodded.

"It's too damned early in the morning to be filling out paperwork on a bunch of minor in possession charges," she said, nodding. "Besides, what are the odds they don't hear us coming, anyway?"

"Not great," he admitted. He led the way down a narrow trail, doing a much better job of moving quietly than she was. Be a miracle if they're not all holding up glasses of milk and singing "How Dry I Am" when they got there, she thought. She could see the glow of a bonfire up ahead and to the left, and Wendall nodded.

"Guess we found 'em," he said.

"Let's get it over with," she said, stepping forward. She turned the corner, and Wendall almost ran over her as she stopped in her tracks.

"Mother of God," Wendall said behind her as her brain tried to translate what she was seeing into something that made sense.

A large circular platform had been built in the middle of the clearing. The bonfire they'd seen sat in the middle, and the glow it cast sent shadows from the bodies swinging slowly from ropes around the perimeter onto the pine trees.

"My God," she said, struggling not to break down crying as her mind methodically counted the bodies hanging from the scaffold. There were twenty of them, all obviously high school kids. Some of the boys wore letter jackets, their brass football and basketball pins glinting in the firelight as the ropes creaked under their weight.

"Chief?" Wendall said, and it took her a moment to understand why he sounded so different; he was shaken, almost crying as he surveyed the scene. "What the hell is this?"

"Call Earl," she said, trying to get herself together. "We're going to need someone in the station. Tell him I need the medical examiner. Go on," she said gently, and he nodded, heading back to the first clearing to get better reception.

She was just standing there, looking at the impossible scene and wondering where the hell she was supposed to even start when her own phone rang. The signal was spotty, but she could understand Earl just fine.

"Chief? What the holy hell's going on? I just had Wendall call me up, barely able to put two words together. Swear to God, I think he was crying."

"He probably was," she said, looking at the bodies. "It's pretty bad."

"Not another wreck," he said, and Dana shook her head.

"No," she said. "It's—shit, I don't know what to call it. I need you running the station for me; we're going to be getting a lot of calls in the next few hours."

"I'm on my way," he said. "You want me to call the boys in?"

"First call the ME, and tell him I need everyone he's got out at Hanger's Woods," she said, and almost groaned as she said it; the irony was horrible. "Then call everyone in. I'm afraid it's an all hands on deck kind of a night."

Earl ended the call abruptly, probably to throw on clothes and race in to the station. She stood there for a moment, wondering how she was going to break the news to the families.

One at a time, she told herself. It wasn't the first time she'd done difficult notifications, but she'd never had to do so many before. Standing alone in the clearing and looking at what was apparently a mass suicide, she let go and cried quietly as she dialed Macy's number to let her know she wouldn't be home before morning.

****

By the time Wendall came back carrying two large rolls of crime scene tape, she'd more or less gotten herself together. She was helping him get the tape up when Mark and Travis came running down the path. Wendall turned quickly, hand going to his weapon, and she put a hand on his arm to stop him as they pulled up short.

"Jesus, Mary, and Joseph," Mark said, looking pale as he

saw what was happening.

"Sorry," Wendall said. "Guess I'm a little jumpy."

"We're all jumpy right now," she said, and the others nodded. "Now's the time to get it together and do the job, fellas. We can fall apart later." Everyone nodded to show they understood.

"Wendall, you go up to the main road and make sure the ME gets here," she said. She didn't like the distant look in his eyes, or the way he'd reached for his weapon so quickly. "Travis, you want to take over for him?"

"Sure thing, Chief," he said, taking the roll of tape from Wendall. They finished taping off the scene.

"Mark, you want to grab the camera, start shooting?" she said, and he nodded, unable to take his eyes off the horrible sight in front of them. After a moment, she snapped her fingers in front of his face, breaking his trance.

"Hey," she said. "Listen, you've got to get it together," she said. "I know it's horrible. It's the worst goddamn thing I've ever seen, and that's saying something. But we have to keep it together, or we're never gonna get through this. Now, can you do this, or do I need to send you back to the station and get Earl to cover for you?"

"I'm good," he said. "Sorry, Chief. It's just—I know some of these kids. Hell, I know all of them."

"So do I," she said. "We all do. But we've got a job to do. Now, go grab the camera out of Wendall's car, and let's get to work. I want pictures of everything. Every angle, every detail. If you're not a thousand percent sure, shoot it. Understand?"

"Yes ma'am," he said, and went to do as he was told.

"He gonna be okay?" Travis said, looking a little shaken himself.

"He either will, or he won't," she said. "We don't have time to babysit him right now. How about you? You good?"

"Not by a long damn shot," he said, shaking his head. "But I'm here. What do you need me doing?"

"Preliminary IDs," she said. "I need a list of names."

"On it," he said, taking out his notebook and looking

thankful for some direction. After a bit of hesitation, he climbed up the steps to the platform and started writing down names as he looked at faces.

Mark came back, carrying the camera and looking like he might possibly have his shit together. He started shooting as soon as he walked into the clearing, and she was oddly thankful she'd managed to upgrade to digital when she took over, or otherwise they'd probably use up half the year's budget on film for this. She would probably have at least a thousand pictures to get through, but too many was better than missing something that might be important to save film.

"Chief, ME's here," Wendall said over the radio. Shit, she thought.

"Aw hell," Travis said, understanding what was happening immediately. She could probably go door to door through the whole town, and not come up with a dozen people who didn't either own an actual scanner or have a scanner app, which meant everyone who happened to be listening in would be calling everyone who wasn't and telling them something was going on. "We're about to be up to our asses in it, aren't we?" he said.

"It's the middle of the night," she said. "Maybe we'll get lucky." Her phone beeped with a message. She nodded as she saw the mass text from the station's computer system, advising all officers to avoid using the radio until further notice.

"Earl's on it, anyway," Travis said, holding up his own phone. "Five'll get you twenty he's chewing Wendall a new one over the phone right now."

"I hope not," she said. "We've got enough problems right now."

CHAPTER FOUR

The ME and a small army of assistants came into the clearing. Walter Howe was a tall, broad-shouldered, and thoroughly intimidating man of indeterminate age, although he'd been the medical examiner for at least twenty years. He ran his department like an Army unit, and when he said "frog," everyone around him jumped without asking how high.

"Chief," Walt said as he walked into the clearing. "What is so—Jesus Christ," he said, stopping in mid-rant. All of his assistants stopped short at the sight of anything that could shock Walt into silence.

"Doc," she said, thankful for the chance to look away for a moment. "Sorry to get you out of bed."

"To hell with that," he said, shaking his head. "Shit on a cracker. They're just kids."

"Seniors," she said. "Travis is getting preliminary IDs, but I need positive identifications just as soon as you can."

"Figured as much," he said. "We treating this like what it

looks like?" he said, and she shook her head.

"We treat it just like what it is, a bunch of unexplained bodies," she said. "Until you tell us differently, anyway."

"Gonna be a bitch of a day, isn't it?" he said, and she nodded.

"Sure looks that way," she said.

"Perkins, McGuire," he said, and two of his assistants stepped forward. If either one of them was much older than the kids in front of her, she'd eat her holster. "Go back and bring out the other van, and we're going to need a lot more bags."

"Yes sir," one of them said, and they left, looking grateful to be gone. She didn't blame them; she wanted to turn around and run away as fast as she could, too.

"Well, come on," he said to the others. "Get what bags we have laid out." They laid out all three body bags they'd brought near the bottom of the stairs as Walt walked up the steps. She went with him.

"Chief, I know it might be in bad taste, but I'm supposed to be training these yahoos," he said quietly. "You mind if I use the opportunity?"

"Everyone's gotta learn sometime," she said. "Just make sure they understand what they're dealing with."

"Won't be a problem," he said. She wandered around the platform as they gather around him, and started looking for anything that didn't belong.

"I know it's rough," Walt said to the gathered group, "but if you're going to do this job, you're going to see a lot worse. Now's not the time to be squeamish. Now's the time to do our job so we can do right by these poor souls."

She couldn't have put it better herself, she thought as Walt walked them through the process of determining the best way to get the bodies down with minimal disturbance.

The ropes were looped over high cross beams and tied off to the platform. "Shouldn't we just cut them down?" someone said, and Walt shook his head.

"Not until we know how we're going to do it right," he said. "And we'll do it the exact same way every time. Listen up, because this is important. We don't rush. We take our time, go slow, and we get it right."

"Make sure you preserve those knots for me," Dana said, and he nodded.

"Hear that? When we do get them down, we're going to cut well away from the knots. Now, I want two of you up here, and the rest of us on the ground," he said. The bodies were hanging about a foot from the ground, and their heads were actually well below the platform itself.

"Chief, you see this, right?" he said as he stepped into the middle of the opening, and she nodded. She looked at the platform itself; it was well constructed and sturdy, and at least fifteen feet off the ground.

"Whoever built this knew what they were doing," she said.

"Most people who hang themselves, or someone else, don't really know what the hell they're doing," he said to his students. "They end up strangling instead of hanging. This damned thing was built with hanging in mind. Drop is more than enough to snap the neck."

"See anything off on any of the bodies?" Dana asked as she looked down, and Walt took a look at each one, studying it carefully.

"Hard to be sure until the post, but I don't see any ligature marks or defensive wounds," he said, inspecting the hands of one of the larger boys. "No scrapes or bruising on the knuckles."

"That's Chase Garner," Travis said. "Starting linebacker. Tough kid. Anyone would have fought back, it'd be him."

"I don't recognize the girl," Dana said, looking at the petite girl next to him.

"Soo Jung Kim," Walt said. "Her daddy bought the old hardware store when Mickey retired last year."

"Sir, should we get started?" one of the two still on the platform asked. Walt shook his head.

"We'll wait for the rest of the bags and the other van," he said. "I want to do all of it at the same time. Meanwhile, we take a look at what we can, look for anything that doesn't belong."

Dana stepped down off the platform and walked over to

Mark, who was keeping himself busy shooting pictures of the platform. "Pay attention to the construction," she said. "Look at these joints."

"Nice and tight," he said. "Chief, I don't think this was slapped together by a bunch of kids."

"Neither do I," she said. "Question is, who built it?"

"I could put in a call to Ed Hackney out at the lumberyard," he said. "See who's bought enough lumber for a project this big lately."

"Good idea," she said. "First, go through the pictures, pick out good shots of the construction. No bodies in them, and don't tell him what's happened just yet."

"He's gonna hear it sooner or later," Mark said. "Hell, everyone in town will probably know by lunch. You know this town."

"I do," she said, "but I'd like to make sure their families don't hear about it at the lunch counter at Kelley's. We keep it tight until the notifications are done."

"Yes ma'am," he said.

"Go on," she said. "Travis?"

"Chief," he said, walking over to her. "Got that list for you." He handed her the notebook, his hands shaking ever so slightly. She read over the list of twenty names, most of which seemed entirely too familiar to her.

"Get with Walt, see if he agrees. And better grab a fire extinguisher," she said, looking at the bonfire. "I don't want anything burning up."

"Yes ma'am," he said. He took the notebook over to where Walt was walking his students through the process of a visual inspection of the body, and they conferred for a moment. Walt walked around the circle, nodding at each body.

"Look right to you, Walt?" she said, and he nodded.

"I'll give you more once they're down," he said, "but he's got it right."

"Go ahead and grab that fire extinguisher," she said, and Travis nodded, actually running for the car. It was stupid; it should have been the first thing she'd done. God only knew what evidence might have been burning up in front of her this whole time, but she didn't have time to beat herself up now.

Something told her she was going to be beat up plenty by the time this day was over.

****

The sun was up by the time the last of the bodies was taken down and driven away. Dana stood at the base of the stairs to the platform, looking at the structure and wondering where it had come from. She was sure about one thing; Mark was right. This wasn't built hastily or slapped together without a plan. It took knowledge and experience to build anything this solid.

"Walt say what he thinks happened out here?" Wendall said, and she shook her head.

"Does he ever?" she said. "He's thorough. He'll want to wait until the autopsies to be sure."

"Be interested to see the tox results," Wendall said, and she nodded. It would be damned near impossible to control a group of people long enough to hang them all, even with lots of guns. Odds were someone would have been shot, and there was no evidence of that, either here or in the first clearing. No blood, no shells, no stray bullets in nearby trees.

"You and me both," she said.

"You hear back from the state lab boys yet?" he said, and she nodded.

"According to them, apparent suicides are low priority," she said. "Doc rules any of them suspicious, and they'll get someone out here."

"Meantime it's gonna rain, and anything resembling forensic evidence gets washed away," he said. "Figures."

"You've been on for what, seventeen hours now? Go get some sleep," she said. "Mark can finish up here."

"I'm good," he said, but she shook her head.

"You know better," she said. "You're pushing the limits now. You're already on edge. Go get some sleep, come back fresh."

"Yes ma'am," he said, nodding. She wanted to tell him to

35

stop calling her ma'am, for fuck's sake, but she had bigger problems.

"Mark, you've got the scene," she said, and he nodded. "Go over the whole damned thing, top to bottom."

"What are we looking for?" Travis said.

"What are the odds whoever built this didn't hurt himself at least once?" she said. "You're looking for blood, hair, anything we can match. Looks like we've been bumped to the bottom of the list by the state lab, so it's on us. Go slow, look at everything. If you're not sure if you should collect it, then collect it."

"We got it," Travis said as her phone began beeping with text messages. They were from one of Walt's assistants; he refused to use text messaging for any reason. One by one, each message came through with a name and the words "ID CONFIRMED."

"Where will you be?" Mark asked.

"I'll stop by the office and put on a fresh uniform," she said. "Then I'll be doing notifications."

"Let us help with that," Travis said. "That's twenty notifications, Chief."

"I need you guys out here," she said, shaking her head.

"Maybe let Earl give you a hand?" Mark suggested. As ideas went, it wasn't horrible; he at least had experience doing them. But he wasn't exactly known for his gentle approach.

"We'll see," she said. "Get cracking, and don't skip an inch."

"Yes ma'am," they both said in unison, and she shook her head as she started the walk back to her car. She sat behind the wheel, resisting the urge to catch a nap as she dialed the station house. Earl answered on the fourth ring.

"Earl, do I still have a clean uniform hanging in the closet?" she asked.

"Afraid not, and you're gonna want to put one on before you come in," he said quietly. "I've got a whole lot of families in here, asking questions I ain't ready to answer."

"Shit," she said. "Okay. I know it's asking a lot, but just stall them for me. I'll swing by the house and get dressed, and I'll come talk to them."

"Don't spare the horses," Earl said, his voice low. "It's gonna get ugly here soon. Some idjit let the cat outta the bag."

"God damn it," she said harshly.

"Want me to call Walt, see who's been blabbing?" he said, and she was sorely tempted to tell him yes.

"No," she said. "It's not important. Have any of them figured it out yet?"

"I don't think they want to," he said. "I think most of them are here waiting for you to tell them everything's okay."

"Okay," she said. "I'll be there in fifteen."

"Better make it ten," he said. "Pretty sure no one will ticket you for speeding."

CHAPTER FIVE

She parked the cruiser at the curb and ran into the house, a little sad to realize Macy must have gone to work. Of course she had; school was in session, and there were bound to be a lot of confused, shaken students. Probably more than a few faculty as well, she realized. She wished she could stop by and see how she was doing, but there was no time.

She cleaned up and put on a fresh dress uniform; somehow learning your loved one was dead came a little easier from someone in a sharp uniform. She didn't understand it, but she'd seen it in action. Her old mentor back in Amarillo when she'd first made detective had made a point of changing into his dress uniform when he had to do a notification, and the habit had rubbed off on her.

She stopped to put her hat on straight, thinking she was about to do more notifications in one day than she had in her entire career. She put the thought out of her mind and locked up the house.

She was pulling into her designated parking space at the

back of the station when she saw someone waiting for her at the back door. At first she thought it was just Earl stepping out back for a smoke, but she dismissed it immediately; Earl would never leave a group of people alone in the station, especially with someone in the tank.

Mayor Patrick Shelby was a thoroughly unpleasant man once you got to know him, something she'd been unable to avoid. He smelled like the cheap cigars he smoked almost constantly, and his demeanor could most kindly described as rude. The man was an insufferable ass on a good day, and this was far from a good day.

"Chief," he said. She briefly considered just walking over him, but stopped at the last minute instead. "Are the rumors I'm hearing true?"

"I have no way of knowing what rumors you're hearing," she said.

"Did half the goddamn senior class of this town just commit suicide?" he said harshly.

"We found multiple bodies in the woods," she said. "The medical examiner is just beginning his examinations, so cause of death has yet to be determined."

"Cut the crap," he said. "I need to know what this was."

She supposed she could have been more polite, or at least more professional, but she wasn't. She was tired, emotionally and physically, and her heart hurt from what she'd been staring at all night.

"Mr. Mayor," she said harshly. "I'm beyond tired. I'm fucking exhausted. I've just spent the night looking at twenty some dead kids. Now I have twenty sets of parents waiting for me inside. They need to know what happened. You're just here to make sure none of this can bite you in the ass, and maybe make sure you're seen showing concern. Neither of which I give a shit about right now, so if you'll excuse me," she said, stepping past him and into the station before he could stop sputtering long enough to respond.

Earl met her at the back door. "That little rat bastard try to corner you?" he said, and she nodded.

"Pretty sure I just got myself removed from his Christmas card list," she said. "Are all of the parents here?"

"Had them all sign in, checked it against the list Walt faxed over while no one was looking."

"We don't have a sign-in procedure," she said, nodding her approval. "That's good work."

"Seemed better than asking them all one by one," he said.

"Anyone more vocal than anyone else?" she asked, and he shook his head.

"I've been thinking," he said. "You weren't here for it, but back in '92 we had a bus crash coming back from the state volleyball championships. Real goddamn mess; eight dead, seventeen wounded. I gather by the look on your face you're thinking of telling them individually. I tried the same. Didn't make it to the second one before they all knew something was wrong, and started hollering like the devil for answers. My advice? Talk to them all at once first. Get it out of the way, and then confirm each one as they come to talk to you."

"There are days when I think you should still be wearing this," she said, tapping her badge.

"Shit, no," he said. "I did my time. But I'm here to help if you need anything."

"Appreciate it," she said. She started for the main office, but stopped. "You know any good carpenters? I mean damned good."

"A few," he said. "You looking to do some work on the house?"

"Not really," she said. "Think you could get me a list of the best?"

"Sure thing," he said. She nodded, then took off her hat and stepped into the office, trying not to cringe at the press of the crowd gathered there.

✳✳✳

Eventually the last set of grieving parents, Jack and Leslie Garner, left to go to the morgue for the identification, and she collapsed in a chair across from Earl's desk.

"That fucking sucked," she said, and he nodded.

"Never gets any easier," he said. "You handled it well."

40

She groaned as the phone rang, and Earl shooed her away from it as he answered it.

"Police department," he said. "One moment. I said just a moment," he barked, putting a hand over the receiver. "It's that damnable pest from the paper," he said. "Romero. She's been calling all morning, wants a statement."

"I don't suppose telling her to roll it in a ball would be professional?" she said, and he gave her a sad laugh.

"Not really, which is probably why I'd do just that," he said. "Want me to tell her to call back?"

"No," she said, getting up slowly. "I'll take it in my office." She trudged to her office door and collapsed into her chair, staring at the phone in resentment for a moment before picking it up.

"Miss Romero," she said. "Chief Atwater."

"Chief, I was hoping to get a statement from you concerning the tragic events of last night," she said.

"I'll tell you what I can," she said. "But not over the phone."

"Certainly," Romero said. "I can come to you, if that would be easier."

"That will be fine," she said, suddenly wishing she had a cot in here. Thinking of cots reminded her of Jason Hill, and she refrained from cursing out loud. "Give me half an hour."

"I'll be there," she said. Dana hung up and let her head sink to the desk for a minute, suddenly afraid this day was about to get a lot worse.

"Earl," she said, stepping out of her office. She looked over at the cell, which was empty and the bed made. "What happened to him?" she said, pointing at the empty cell.

"Figured we had bigger fish to fry than his sorry butt," he said. "Hope I didn't overstep, but you did say you'd have him out in time for work, and I didn't really want him running his mouth while all them folks were here."

"No, it's fine," she said. "Was he sober when he left?"

"He was when I was done talking to him," Earl said, and she was suddenly sure she didn't want to know what that particular conversation had entailed. She had no doubt that

Hill, dumb as he might be, had behaved himself completely until he was well out of sight of the station. Back in his day, Earl had been known to make grown men wet themselves, and she doubted he'd lost much of his touch.

"Well, maybe we'll get lucky and we won't hear from him for a while," she said.

"When are we ever lucky?" he said, and she shrugged.

"It could happen, right?" she said.

"You gonna talk to that reporter?" he said, and she nodded with a sigh.

"All the victims have been identified and the families notified," she said. "No harm in telling her what I can. Maybe someone sees the article and comes forward to tell us they'd been planning something like this."

"You think it was a mass suicide?" he said. There was a gleam in his eye that said he wasn't any more convinced than she was, and he hadn't even been on the scene.

"Nothing about the bodies to tell me otherwise," she said. "No defensive wounds or any sign they'd been restrained or subdued. Some of the boys were pretty big, too."

"But you're not convinced, are you?" he said, honing in on exactly what was bugging her. It was the primary reason she kept him around; he might be getting old, but creaky joints didn't affect his instincts.

"Honestly, I don't know what to think," she said. "You should have seen this platform, Earl. I don't know a lot about carpentry, but I can tell you whoever built it knew what they were doing. It sure as hell wasn't put up by a bunch of kids."

"Speaking of," he said, handing her a sheet of paper. "Best carpenters in the county. List is best to worst, so I'd start at the top. Even if they didn't build it, they might be able to point you in the right direction."

"Really?" she said, and he nodded.

"Carpentry's as much art as science," he said. "Man does it long enough, he develops his own style. Works a lot like a signature. I'd bet some of them will recognize it."

"I'll go see them as soon as I'm done with this," she said as Lisa Romero walked into the station.

"Good luck," he said quietly. "Woman's a damned piranha in a skirt."

"Chief," Romero said, and Dana nodded.

"Get you anything? Coffee?" she said as she led her back to her office.

"No thank you," she said, smiling pleasantly. It seemed wrong, but she managed not to tell her to wipe that fucking grin off her face. She realized, not for the first time, that it was going to be a very long day.

"As I'm sure you can understand," Romero said, pulling out her digital recorder, "rumors are flying. I'd like to get the facts from you."

"Well, here's what we know. At about midnight last night, officers responded to several missing persons calls. After collecting the information, we began a routine check of all the common places students gather, at which time an officer spotted several cars tied to the missing persons reports. I joined the responding officer at the scene, and after a search of the area we found the bodies of twenty individuals."

"Was it a mass suicide?" she said, and Dana shook her head.

"We're still waiting for the medical examiner's reports," she said. "As of right now, cause and manner of death are undetermined, and as a rule I don't speculate."

"Have the victims been positively identified?" she asked, and Dana nodded.

"They have, and the families have been notified," she said, sliding a piece of paper with the names and ages of all the victims over to her. She pointed to the recorder and made a cutting gesture across her throat, and Romero grudgingly turned it off.

"Off the record?" Dana said, and she nodded.

"Of course," she said.

"Good, because if you quote me I'll deny it. Unofficially, I don't see any direct physical evidence that contradicts the suicide theory, but we're just beginning our investigation. This is all very preliminary information, Miss Romero. I'm trusting you to treat the subject delicately."

"I will," she said, looking at the list. "I knew most of these kids, Chief. Trust me, I'm not looking to stir the pot. I just need to tell the town what happened as best I can."

"Then I can trust you not to jump to conclusions until we know more," she said, and Romero nodded. She didn't believe her for a second, but she'd gotten her to agree. It would give her an excuse to cut her out later, after she screwed her over.

Romero stood up, putting her recorder away. The two shook hands. "Thank you for your time, Chief. I know you must be incredibly busy."

"That's an understatement," she said, "but you're welcome. I know this department doesn't have the most sparkling history of cooperation with the press, and I'd like to change that. But I need to be very clear, Miss Romero. I'm an open book, so long as you play it straight. You burn me, and you'll never get another word out of anyone in this department."

"I think we understand each other," Romero said, and Dana nodded. She showed her out, trying not to laugh as Earl rolled his eyes. After she was gone, she stopped at the coffee pot.

"Think she's gonna mud-suck you?" he said, and she nodded.

"First chance she gets," Dana said. "Be surprised if she doesn't print what I told her 'off the record' word for word."

"You want me to call some of those boys, see if they can come in?" he said, and she shook her head.

"Not just yet," she said. "I suppose I should work this like what it probably is. Go talk to their friends, teachers, see if they gave any sort of indication they were suicidal."

"Something stinks," Earl said, and she nodded. "Twenty kids couldn't plan a panty raid without thirty more people knowing about it in this town. Hard to believe they could organize something like this without anyone getting wind of it."

"I know," she said, downing the coffee. "I'll be on my cell if you need me."

"Gotcha," he said. "You want me to check in on Travis

and the kid?"

"They're fine," she said. "Got them going over that platform, looking for anything someone might have left behind."

"That don't take two men," he said, and she nodded. "You made the kid stay out there to get him used to it, didn't you?"

"He's going to have to toughen up a little, or he'll end up on a psych pension," she said.

"Starting to have second thoughts about him?" Earl said, and she shrugged.

"I don't know yet," she said. "Guess it's up to him." She rapped her knuckles on his desk. "Hold the fort. I'll be at the high school."

CHAPTER SIX

She checked in at the office, not at all surprised to see everyone looked like they'd been crying, even the vice principal, Henry MacNeil.

Just down the hall was the guidance counselor's office, which looked to be the busiest room in the school. Several students were waiting to speak to her. Most of them were either crying or staring off into the distance. She braced herself for the questions they would no doubt have for her, but thankfully they mostly ignored her.

As she waited, she texted Mark to see if they were still at the scene. He replied that they'd just cleared, and were pulling into the station now.

She dialed his number, stepping away from the students to speak quietly. "Mark, I need you to send me the pictures you took of the platform," she said.

"Just the platform?" he said.

"Yes, and make damned sure that's all that's in them," she said.

"Gotcha. Give me two minutes to get to a computer," he said. She thanked him and hung up, and sure enough her phone vibrated with new messages. She downloaded the images and scrolled through them to make sure they were safe, and by the time she was done the guidance counselor was ready to speak with her.

Melody Hagerrman was a short, somewhat plain-looking blonde woman in her late thirties. She seemed to be holding up a little better than some of the other faculty she'd seen so far, but she supposed she had to at least appear to be okay if she was going to help students through all this.

"Chief," Hagerrman said, holding her door open. Dana stepped through, and she closed the door behind them before sitting down at her desk. "I've got a few minutes I can spare, but as I'm sure you can imagine I'm swamped."

"I won't take up much of your time," Dana said. "You knew the victims, I take it?"

"It's a pretty small class," she said. "I'm pretty familiar with most of them on one level or another."

"Did any of them give you any sort of indication they were in trouble?" Dana said. "Trouble with grades, personal problems, maybe problems with other students?"

"Nothing severe comes to mind," she said. "It's high school, which pretty much automatically means almost everything is life-or-death."

"Any troubles with bullying? Maybe drugs or alcohol abuse?" she said, watching for her reaction more than listening for her answer.

"Again, nothing immediately comes to mind," she said. "You know what kids are like. There are always outcasts, but they all seemed to be pretty well-adjusted. A few romantic squabbles here and there. And sure, most of them had their share of beers at parties and such, but I can't recall anyone who seemed to be having a problem functioning. I pulled their files this morning," she said, tapping a stack of file folders. "Grades all seem to be within the normal range. Couple of failed classes here and there, but nothing that couldn't be remedied with a little hard work."

"Did they all run together?" she said. "Anyone there you

were surprised to see in the group?"

"Janelle Stuart sticks out a little," she said, pulling a file from the stack. "She was a sophomore, but she was dating one of the seniors, so it's not all that unusual she'd be with him."

"Say I needed to talk to their friends," Dana said. "How would I make that happen?"

"I'm not sure," she said, and for the first time her cool, collected exterior cracked just a bit. "Most of their friends were with them."

"Anyone who wasn't?" Dana said, and she nodded. "Seems like a lot of upset students waiting to talk to you if all their friends are dead."

"Some of them are just upset enough to miss class," she said, sounding incredibly cynical. "There are a few who are just genuinely shaken by the whole thing, though."

Dana nodded, noticing she hadn't actually answered the question. "So, no real indicators any of them were in any sort of trouble. No bullying or personal problems?"

"I wish there was something there to give you," she said. "Honestly, I probably shouldn't say this, but if I were making a list of students likely to do something like this, I doubt any of their names would end up on it."

"So, if they didn't have problems, maybe the problem was with someone else? Anyone who might have had an issue with them?" She watched as the woman squirmed, straightening her desk blotter. She was nervous, and Dana knew she was onto something.

"Now's not the time to hold back," Dana said. "If you know something, you need to tell me. I've got twenty dead kids, and so far the only explanation is a mass suicide that makes no sense."

"There was a boy," she said. "A little older than them, but he'd been held back because he missed a lot of school when he was younger. Medical problems. He was badly injured in a fire."

"What was his name?" she said.

"I'm not sure I can--"

"Ma'am, I'm not particularly inclined to be polite about

this right now," she said. "I want his name. I can get it other ways, but I'd rather you make this easier on all of us and just tell me his name, and what sort of problems there were between him and these kids."

"You have to understand, he was—is, a very damaged young man. Most of his body is heavily scarred, and he's suffered tremendous psychological trauma. He lost his father in the same fire that scarred him. You know how kids can be about anyone who looks different. Even good kids can be cruel."

Dana stared her down for a minute, and she blinked first. "Gavin Anderson," Hagerrman said finally. "He dropped out at the beginning of the year."

"Thank you," she said.

***

The counselor might have been less than cooperative, but she was pretty sure she knew at least one teacher who'd open up to her.

She found Macy's classroom, standing outside the door as she waited for class to end. The bell rang, and only six students filed out. It took her a moment to understand why; most of the victims had probably been in the class.

"Hey," she said, stepping into the classroom. "Rough day."

"Yes, it is," Macy said. She looked like she needed a hug, but she respected Dana's rule about PDA, particularly when she was in uniform. Screw it, Dana thought, and touched her hand. It wasn't enough, but it would have to do.

"They keep asking me if I know what happened," Macy said, looking out at the empty seats. "I don't know what to tell them. Did they all really kill themselves?"

"I don't know yet," Dana said. "It sure looks that way on the surface, but I have some questions I need to put to bed before I call it."

"So this isn't a social visit," Macy said, visibly upset. Dana felt like utter crap about it, but she had a job to do. Macy knew who she was when this all started, and that wasn't

49

about to change now.

"What do you know about a kid named Gavin Anderson?" she asked.

"You've been talking to Hagerrman," she said, and Dana nodded.

"Practically had to drag the name out of her," she said.

"Bright kid," she said. "No, not just bright. A damn genius, is what he is. Smarter than I am, at any rate, and he knew it. Poor kid. I tell you, if there's ever been someone who deserved a freaking break, it was Gavin. Lost his dad, ended up covered in scars. You know kids," she said, and Dana nodded.

"Any of the victims ever give him problems?" she said. "Maybe bullied him, harassed him?"

"Everyone gave Gavin problems," she said. "Half the damned teachers in this place didn't treat him any better than the students. Teachers don't always react well when they figure out one of their students is smarter than they are."

"That include the counselor?" she asked, and Macy nodded, looking angry.

"Oh, he drove her nuts. She tried to shrink him every way she could think of, and he just led her around by the nose. You bet your ass she resented it. You don't think Gavin could have had anything to do with this? I mean, yes. He's got some real problems. But I don't see him hurting anyone."

"Right now I don't think anything," Dana said. "I just need to run down everything." She touched her hand again, pulling it back quickly as the first students for her next class came through the door.

"Couple of these kids were pretty tight with some of them," Macy said, putting on her best professional face. "Might be worth your time to talk to them."

"You don't mind?" she said, and Macy shook her head.

"We're all sort of on autopilot," she said. "I doubt there's been much teaching happening so far." The students filed in and took their seats, uncharacteristically quiet for teenagers.

"Class, this is Chief Atwater. She has some questions she needs to ask. It's okay if you don't know the answers, but if you do, it would be very helpful if you could share them."

"Thank you," she said, nodding to Macy. "Were any of you close to any of the victims?"

One girl raised her hand. "I hung out with Soo Jung sometimes," she said. "She was teaching me Korean, and I helped her with her history."

"Good friends?" Dana asked, and she nodded. "Was there anything going on in her life, anything that was upsetting her or making things difficult?"

"No," she said. "That's the thing. She was happy. Her grades were great, she got along great with her parents. She had colleges recruiting her left and right. Even had a crush on a guy."

"Chase Garner," someone else said.

"And was it mutual?" Dana asked.

"Guy wouldn't shut up about her," the kid said, and there were a few muted laughs from some of the other boys.

"Okay," Dana said, nodding. "Folks, I need to say something. When something like this happens, it almost never makes any sense. Things can get confusing, and sometimes it can drive us to do something we normally wouldn't do. If you're having problems, at school or at home, or anywhere, please talk to someone. I know Miss Macy's door is always open," she said, and Macy nodded.

"Talk to someone, please," Dana said. "Your parents, friends, teachers, guidance counselors, someone. Please," she said. "If you're not comfortable talking to any of these people, you can always come find me. I promise you I'll listen."

Several of the students nodded. Dana felt like there was more she should say, but she didn't know what it would be.

"Thank you, Chief," Macy said. "Everyone, if you'll take out your materials, we'll get started in just a moment." Dana let her lead her out of the classroom, standing in the empty hallway.

"That was a good thing you just did," she said, and Dana shrugged.

"Feels like too little, too late," she said. "You know the statistics as well as I do."

"I do," Macy said. "And the administration is doing the whole full-court press. Most of us are spending the day just trying to get them to talk. But we're all on edge waiting for it."

"Copycats," Dana said, almost afraid to say it. Her own reservations aside, this looked like a mass suicide, and that almost always meant there would be more. Macy looked her over for a minute.

"Something's eating at you," she said. "I know that look."

"Like I said, I have some things I need to clear up," she said. "Um, which way to the shop classes?"

"Down that hall," she said. "Out the side door to the shop building."

"Thank you," Dana said. Screw it, she thought. She gave her a quick hug, and Macy was wiping her cheeks as she pulled away.

"Whatever this is," Macy said, "please figure it out. If those kids did kill themselves, the others need to know why. And if they didn't," she said.

"Someone has to answer for it," Dana said, finishing her thought. She let Macy get back to her students, and went to find the shop teacher. It might be thin, but she had at least two different angles she needed to run down before she was comfortable calling this a suicide.

CHAPTER SEVEN

"Does anything about this strike you as familiar?" Dana asked, showing the shop teacher the images Mark had sent her. He looked at her phone for a moment, shaking his head.

"Not offhand," he said. "Kinda looks like a gazebo. Seems like solid construction, though. Is this—is this where it happened?"

"Yes," Dana said, taking a chance. Her official position had always been to refrain from giving out any information that wasn't vital, but she needed his opinion, and for that he needed to trust her. "I take it you teach drafting classes, as well?"

"I do," he said. "Drafting, construction, and woodshop."

"You ever see anyone draw up anything similar?" she said.

"All the time," he said, shaking his head. "This looks like half the gazebos I see every year. It's one of the projects I use for finals. It's obviously been modified, but it's hardly original."

"Thank you," she said, letting him get back to his students. Rather than go back through the school, where she was liable to be cornered by faculty or students, she walked around the side of the building to the parking lot. She was just about to pull out when her phone rang.

"Chief, it's Walt," he said as soon as she answered.

"You have something for me?" she said.

"Depends on how you look at it," he said. "Now, I ain't had close to enough time to get through all of them, but I've run a few tox screens so far. On the larger boys, you know."

"Makes sense," she said. "If you're gonna drug someone, you drug the dangerous ones."

"That's just it," he said. "There's nothing there. No barbituates or narcotics, no sedatives. Nothing at all that would incapacitate even a small child, let alone a strapping young man. Hell, they didn't even have enough alcohol in their systems to slow them down."

"Okay, then," Dana said. "I don't suppose any bruising developed since we got them down?"

"Not a thing," Walt said. "Chief, awful as it is to think about, I don't see anything here to tell me this was anything but a mass suicide. I'll do the autopsies because it's required by law, but honestly I don't think there's going to be any surprises. Your call, not mine, but I don't see much in the way of a crime here."

"Someone built that platform," she said. "At the least, that's facilitation."

"Maybe," he said. "Or maybe a couple of the boys were a little better at carpentry than we thought. Look, I'm just about to start the posts, and that'll tell us for sure. But I'm inclined to rule these deaths as suicides."

"Okay. Thanks, Walt," she said. "Let me know if you find anything unusual."

"You'll be the first call I make," he said. She let him go and drove away, wondering if she was actually on to something, or just chasing shadows.

***

She made it back to the station without any more distractions, where she was a little surprised to see Travis was still on duty.

"Chief, we went over every visible inch of that damned platform," he said. "If there's a speck of blood or a hair there, we couldn't find it."

"Okay. You should probably go home and get some sleep," she said, patting him on the shoulder. "I need you on tonight." He nodded without arguing and went home as Mark sat at his computer, going through the pictures.

She stood behind him, looking at the screen. "Anything stand out to you?" she said, and he nodded. He opened up several pictures to show her side-by-side.

"Look at the knots," he said. The pictures showed all the nooses. "They're all exactly the same. I know we don't guess, but if I had to, I'd say they were all tied by the same person."

"Okay," she said. "That's something."

"Here's where it gets strange," he said, opening several more pictures. "The nooses are all the same, but look at how they're attached to the platform. I've got at least a dozen different styles of knots here."

"Meaning they were tied down by different people," she said, patting his shoulder. "That's good work."

"Thanks," he said. "But what do we make of it?"

"It's an inconsistency," she said. "Inconsistencies are always important. We have these knots intact?"

"Still wrapped around the wood," he said. "We took the railings off. Everything's labeled."

"Good work," she said again, picking up his phone because it was closest.

"Who are you calling?" he asked.

"State crime lab," she said. "You just gave me probable cause to order forensics testing on the ropes." Mark looked satisfied with himself as she waited for someone to pick up. She eventually got someone on the line, told them who she was, and what she needed. The lab director agreed with her, and said he'd get it in the line.

"I've got twenty bodies in the morgue," she said. "And so far my only theory doesn't necessarily fit the facts. I need a rush on that."

"I'll do what I can," he said. "Best I can promise."

"Thanks," she said, hanging up.

"Now what?" Mark said.

"Now you take one of the patrol cars and drive that evidence up to the state lab in Springfield," she said. "I don't want to wait for a courier. Gas up before you sign it out, and no stops on the way. You sign it in yourself, and then get back here."

"Yes ma'am," he said, standing up and grabbing his hat. She was about to tell him not to call her ma'am when Earl looked up from the phone, snapping his fingers to get her attention.

"We're on the way," he said. "Don't let anyone near them, and don't let anyone leave." He hung up as Dana walked over to his desk.

"What now?" Dana said. Judging by the look on Earl's face, it wasn't good news.

"You need to get out to the cemetery, now," he said, handing her the page from the notebook he used to write down details of calls for service.

"Shit," she said, reading it over. "Is this for real?"

"Chris St. John called it in," Earl said. Chris was the sexton in charge of the cemetery. He was a veteran, and level-headed enough he didn't panic easily. "He doesn't get froggy over nothing."

"I'm on the way," she said.

"You want me with you?" Mark said. She looked at the slip again. It would be nice to have another pair of eyes, but she needed him doing what she told him to do.

"No," she said. "I need that evidence to get to the lab ASAP. Just hustle up."

"I'll call Walt for you," Earl said, looking grim.

"What the hell is going on here?" she said, shaking her head and walking out to her car.

***

56

"Jesus," she said as she looked at the second apparent group suicide in two days. Six bodies lay in a circle in an open section of the cemetery.

"Damnedest thing I've ever seen," Chris said, tilting his hat back. "Chief, I've seen guys blow themselves up, shoot themselves in the head, swallow a handful of pain killers and chase it down with a bottle of whiskey. Even saw a guy that sliced his arms open deep enough to scratch the bone. I've never seen anyone kill themselves like this."

She had to agree. All six bodies were pinned to the ground, impaled on wooden stakes buried in the dirt. The bloody points jutted out their backs, and if she had to guess, each one had gone right through the heart. It was easily the most gruesome thing she'd ever seen.

"Who found them?" she asked.

"I did," Chris said. "Well, me and the guy I hire to help me mow now and then."

"Where is he?" she asked.

"Up at the office," he said. "Hell, he's just a kid himself. Barely old enough to drink. He's pretty shook up."

"Did either of you touch anything?" she asked, and Chris shook his head.

"Called it in right away," he said. "Lucky we found it when we did. If we hadn't been scheduled to mow out this way today, might not have been found for a couple of days."

Dana knelt down next to the closest body, and felt like screaming as she recognized her. It was the girl from Macy's class, the one who'd been friends with the Kim girl. "Shit," she said. She made herself get it under control, and get to work. She examined the body as best she could without moving it.

"Grass stains on the knees," Chris said, and she was a little embarrassed she didn't notice it first.

"They're on the ground," she said, but Chris shook his head.

"You don't get grass stains just by touching the ground," he said. "You gotta move around, break the blades of grass to get stains." He pointed to the knees of his overalls, which were stained in nearly the identical way.

"Spent about a half-hour this morning on my knees, pulling weeds out front," he said. She nodded. A quick check showed the others had the same stains on their knees. They'd all been kneeling before it happened, and an image she didn't much like showed itself.

They'd knelt down and impaled themselves on the stakes. "Think this has anything to do with what happened last night?" Chris asked.

"Hard not to," she admitted. She was saved from further speculation when Walt arrived, this time with only one assistant.

"Lord almighty," he said, surveying the scene. "What are we looking at here?"

"Wish I knew," she said, walking back to the car to get the camera and start documenting the scene.

***

"Check the bodies for bruising," Dana said as Walt and his assistant were cutting the first stake off at the ground. Pulling the bodies off could compromise evidence. "Especially on the backs and the neck."

"You think someone forced them down on the stakes?" Walt said, and she shrugged.

"Take a hell of a lot of force to do that, don't you think?" she said.

"Wouldn't be easy, but it wouldn't be impossible for them to do it themselves, either. All they'd really have to do was throw themselves down, and the point would do the rest."

"Anything special about the stakes?" she asked, and he shook his head.

"Common garden stakes," he said. "Pick 'em up just about anywhere for fifty cents or so apiece."

"You have any string?" she asked out loud. Chris nodded, fetching a ball of twine from his truck.

"Use it to lay out planters and such," he said. She tied one end to a stake and wrapped it around the opposite one, cutting it off and doing the same with the others.

"Laid out perfectly," Walt said. "Perfect circle."

"Seems like a lot of trouble," she said. "How long do you think it took?"

"Not all that much, if you know what you're doing," Chris said. "If I were doing it, I'd have two of them tied together, then just mark it out and dig."

"Okay," she said, standing up and taking several pictures.

"Walt," the assistant said. He held out what looked like an ID card, and she remembered the school had started issuing them last year.

"Check the rest of them," Dana said as Walt handed it over to her.

"Bingo," he said, holding up five more ID cards.

"Takes care of the identifications," Walt said.

"Guess I'd better run them down," she said, wishing this day would just be over already. It was barely two in the afternoon. "Why aren't they in school?" she asked no one in particular.

"Not that hard to ditch," the assistant said. "Used to do it all the time. You can go out the side door to the shop, then hoof it around the building to the parking lot without being seen." Dana nodded; she'd done the same thing just this morning.

"You sound like you speak from experience," Walt said, and he nodded.

"Did my share of it," he admitted.

"You okay, Chief?" Walt said, looking her over. "Looking a little run down."

"Gee, don't you know how to flatter a girl," she said, and he chuckled. "Just tired of telling people their kids are dead."

"I'll get them ready for the identifications," he said quietly, and she nodded. "The ID cards won't cut it for official ID."

"I know," she said. Suddenly sure that if she looked behind her she'd see a line in the grass where her ass was dragging, she went to go clean up and make the family notifications.

CHAPTER EIGHT

"Take a moment if you need," Dana said as the last set of parents stood in the viewing room. When Walt and his assistant wheeled the body in, covered with a sheet, she heard the mother let out a very quiet sigh, then took her husband's hand and nodded. Dana touched the intercom button.

"Go ahead, Walt," she said quietly, preparing herself for another outpouring of grief. After the mother got herself somewhat under control, Dana asked the question she was here for.

"Is this your son?" she said, and the mother sobbed. The father held her close, and nodded.

"That's my boy," he said, choking up. "What happened?"

"We're still figuring that out," Dana said. It took her a moment to remember the boy's name; it had been a long day. "Did Kevin seem at all upset to you over the last few days? Any problems, at home or at school?"

"No," the father said. "Nothing like that. He just got

accepted to Michigan State. What happened to my son?"

Damn it, she thought. Don't make me say it out loud. "We're still investigating, but preliminary examination shows injuries consistent with a self-inflicted wound."

The mother sobbed louder, and he nodded. "Thank you," he said quietly, leading his wife out of the viewing room. Through the glass, she watched as Walt and his assistant, whose name she couldn't seem to remember for the life of her, wheeled Kevin Jansen's body back into the cooler room. She sat down on the small sofa at the back of the room, stifling a yawn as Walt came into the viewing room.

"It's almost seven," Walt said. "You've been going for something like eighteen hours now. Go home and get some sleep, Chief."

"I can't," she said.

"Bull," he said simply. "You're running on fumes. What exactly do you think you're going to accomplish like this? You couldn't solve a two-clue crossword right now."

She wanted to argue that she had too much going on, but the simple truth was she was at a standstill. She was waiting on lab results from the state police, and Walt's postmortem exams. Since she'd be surprised if Walt was still here in twenty minutes, there was nothing left to be done.

Reluctantly, she stood up, trying unsuccessfully to stifle another yawn as Walt pressed a Styrofoam cup of coffee into her hands and showed her the door. "Go home and get some sleep. Doctor's orders."

"You're not my doctor," she said around another yawn.

"No, but I'm the one who'll have to see to you if you crash that damned car and get yourself killed," he said. "I got enough bodies in here as it is."

"Fair enough," she said, shaking herself and downing the cup of lukewarm coffee.

***

She stopped by the station to make sure everything was kosher. The phone systems Earl answered in the daytime had all forwarded to the county 911 center at night, not that there were many calls for service on the night shift.

She stopped in her office long enough to drop off her notebook so she could write up the report first thing in the morning; she'd learned from long experience that if she brought it home, she'd probably forget it in the morning. She was locking up when she heard a familiar voice coming from behind her.

"Long day?" Earl said, leaning against his desk and packing a pipe.

"Just headed home," she said.

"Good," he said. "You need to sleep, or you're going to burn out on us."

"So I keep hearing," she said. "Glad to hear everyone's so concerned."

"We are, you know," he said. "All the guys are worried you're gonna drive yourself into the ground on this thing. All those years in Texas, you ever work something like this?"

"Few multiple homicides," she said. "Mostly gang stuff. One guy who wiped out his family."

"Then you damn well oughtta know by now this is a marathon, not a sprint. You could have just as easily let Wendall do the identifications; he's done it before, and you know he's good with families."

"I caught the call," Dana said, shrugging. "Seemed like the thing to do."

"You didn't catch the call," he said, shaking his head. "You sent Mark on an errand and poached it."

"I needed that evidence to get to the lab," she said, starting to feel mildly defensive. "And I'm not sure I like where this is headed."

"Then fire me," he said simply. "I got my pension, I'll get by just fine."

"You know I can't do that, Earl," she said. "Never mind trying to find a dispatcher on short notice, you're too valuable."

"Then maybe you should take the free advice," he said. "You've got three other men in this department. Use them. If they aren't useful, replace them. But you can't do it all yourself, and frankly you're the only one who thinks you should. You want to take care of your guys, I get that. But you can't hold their hands and baby them along. You gotta take care of yourself, too."

"I'll go right home and get some rest," she said.

"That's good," he said, putting away his tobacco pouch. "But that ain't all I'm talking about. Let the boys do their jobs, and see to yours." He stuck his pipe between his teeth and headed for the door. "Don't mean to bust your butt, Chief. But you're slipping, and people are starting to notice. City council's been waiting for that expense report for six days now. I been holding 'em off as best I could, and I'm sure today bought you some time, but there ain't gonna be a department for you to run if you don't start taking care of business."

"I know," she said.

"Look, unless something breaks tomorrow, you're stuck spinning your wheels. Take the day, get caught up. I'll run down the carpentry angle if it helps."

"You're not an officer any more," she said, and he shrugged.

"So swear me in," he said. "Ain't like you gotta train me."

It might have just been the exhaustion, or the numbness from the horrors of the day, but right then it was the best idea she'd heard in some time. "I can't pay you any more than I am now," she said, and he nodded.

"Ain't about the money," he said. "You need help, and since you won't trust the guys already on your roster, it might as well be me."

"I trust them all," she said, and he smiled.

"You think so?" he said, smiling. "Tell me you weren't about to go check in with Wendall before you went home."

"Nothing wrong with checking on him," she said.

"Except that there isn't a damned thing going on right now," he said. "Chances are decent he's either posted by the bowling alley or just tooling around. Nothing he needs help for."

Damn it, she thought. She really hated it when he did this, mostly because he was almost always right. She did trust the guys with the day-to-day stuff, but she tended to jump in on anything unusual. Not just supervise or coordinate, which was what her actual job was, but take point on it, like today.

She unlocked her office door and opened a desk drawer, pulling out a badge. She made up a commission card and sent it to the printer, then ran it through the laminator as she rooted around until she found what she needed.

She held out the Bible, and Earl put his left hand on it, raising his right. She repeated the oath of office from memory, and Earl confirmed that he swore to uphold it. She handed him the badge and card. "Congratulations, Detective," she said.

"Whatever's going on, it'll get sorted out," he said. "Meantime, why don't you go let a certain school teacher take care of you for a bit?"

"Excuse me?" she said, caught off guard.

"Please," he said with a smile. "How many times a week does a teacher need to talk to the Chief, but never actually does while she's in the office? Seems to know your home number by heart, too. I'm old, not dead."

"I honestly thought no one knew," she said.

"'Course you did," he said. "Everyone wants to think they can keep a secret, even when they can't. Let you in on a little secret of my own." He smiled as he gestured with his pipe. "Ain't no one much gives a damn one way or another. I know I don't."

"Thank you," she said. "For everything."

"Hell, I should be thanking you," he said with a laugh. "Now the next time some idjit like Jason Hill shows his ass, I get to kick it."

Lord help me, she thought. What have I unleashed on this town?

"Well, try to keep the body count to a minimum," she said.

"No promises," he said with a grin. "Been too quiet for too long."

"Good night, Earl," she said, laughing and shaking her head as she headed for the back door.

✳✳✳

She was a little surprised to see Macy's car still parked at the school as she drove by. She pulled the patrol car in and parked, knocking at the gymnasium door when she heard voices. Henry MacNeil let her in, putting a finger to his lips as she stepped inside.

"What's going on?" she whispered.

"'Emergency school board meeting'," he said, rolling his eyes. "Basically they've been trying to convince each other they're doing everything they should."

She'd never had much reason to get involved with the school board, since she had no children, but she still knew who they were; it was a small town.

Gary White, the school board president, was talking at great length about setting up a large memorial service for the students. She listened as he went on for a bit, then turned the floor over to Melody Hagerrman, who proceeded to explain how it would help the students to process and grieve.

"Unbelievable," someone said from the floor, and she had to smile as Macy stood up. "We've been screaming at the top of our lungs for two years that we need more resources for student health and safety, and every year we get turned down so the gym can get a makeover, or you guys can vote yourselves a raise. I guess all it takes to loosen the purse strings is a lot of dead students."

"Order," Gary said, looking flustered. "I'll have order."

"Just imagine what we could have done if you'd been willing to spend some of this time and resources on these kids before they killed themselves," Macy said, and stormed off. She hadn't gone three steps before the applause started, and by the time she stepped past Dana and out the door, the meeting had lost all semblance of control.

Dana slipped out to find Macy standing by the door, smoking with one trembling hand. "I know, I know," she said, looking at the cigarette. "These things will kill me."

"Not my place to say anything," she said.

"Isn't it?" Macy said, and Dana let it go. She was too

damned tired to get into it with her girlfriend over her commitment issues. She shook her head. "I'm sorry. I'm just so goddamn frustrated."

"I can see that," she said. "For what it's worth, you weren't wrong in there. End of the day, they're just politicians. Only thing they care about is how the public sees them."

"It doesn't make any sense, Dana," she said. "I knew these kids. None of them showed any of the signs. It just doesn't make sense."

"I've worked a few suicides," Dana said. "They almost never make sense. I think that's why they hit us so hard. It's not just the loss; it's the confusion."

"There's something wrong here, isn't there?" she said. "You can see it, I know you can. Something's not right." She butted the smoke and took a deep breath. She started for the door, rapping lightly on the steel. Henry opened the door, and the sounds of arguing flooded out into the parking lot. "Nice talking to you, Chief," she said, keeping up appearances for her sake.

Fuck it, Dana thought. She was tired, and she felt weighed down by all the death and stupid, senseless loss of it all. Maybe she was just tired of keeping up appearances, especially now that someone she loved was obviously in pain. Whatever the reason for it, it was long overdue.

She stepped forward, pulled Macy into a hug, and then kissed her, not giving a single damn that most everyone inside could plainly see them.

"What are you doing?" Macy said as the kiss broke. "They'll see."

"Let 'em see," she said. She kissed her again. "I'll probably be dead to the world in half an hour, but you're welcome to come by if you don't want to be alone any more than I do tonight."

"I'll be there," she said, kissing her lightly. "But I think right now I'd better go make sure I still have a job."

"They fire you, and I'll just have to stop looking the other way on a lot of things they think I don't know about," she said with a wink. MacNeil let out a polite cough, but nodded his approval.

"They want to get rid of anyone for telling the truth, they'll have to start with me," he said, and Macy nodded. She held onto Dana's hand for a minute, then went back inside.

"You really have something on any of them?" he asked, and she shrugged.

"Everyone's got secrets," she said. "Just have to know how to look." MacNeil nodded, and let the door close as she walked to the car and drove home.

CHAPTER NINE

She woke up with Macy sound asleep beside her. The alarm clock said it was three in the morning. She checked her phone for messages, unusually relieved to find none, and lay back down, one arm around Macy's waist as she listened to her steady breathing.

When it became clear she wasn't going to get back to sleep, she climbed gently out of bed and slipped downstairs, starting a pot of coffee. As she waited for it to brew, she grabbed her laptop and sat down on the couch. The next two hours went by in a blur as she read about terms like "contagion" and "suicide clusters," and by the time she put the computer down, she had a knot in her stomach that wouldn't go away. If the experts were to be believed, they could expect more before everything was said and done. She did her best to put it out of her mind and went upstairs to get ready; the parade was later this morning, and she had work to do.

By the time she came back downstairs and buckled on her

duty belt, Macy was curled up on the couch with a cup of coffee. "Back at it?" she said, and Dana nodded.

"The hours might be long, but at least the pay sucks," she said, and Macy smiled. "You going to the parade later?"

"I suppose," she said. "I don't know, seems wrong somehow."

"I know," Dana said. "Fucked up as it is, life goes on, whether we think it should or not. I still have a department to run, you still have classes to teach. It's enough to make me sick sometimes."

"This helps," she said, holding her hand. "About last night. I'm sorry if I was hard on you."

"No more than I had coming," she said, sitting down next to her. "I'm the one who should be apologizing. None of this has been fair to you, and honestly I wouldn't have blamed you if you'd said 'to hell with it' a long time ago."

"I wasn't always out, you know," she said. "I remember how hard it can be. And it's not like I expect you to grope me in public, but I won't deny that a little acknowledgment would go a long way."

"You're not wrong," Dana said. "Which is why I think we should have dinner tonight."

"Sure," Macy said. "Your place or mine?"

"No," she said. "I mean dinner. Like in a restaurant."

"You're sure?" Macy said. "I mean, I like the sound of that, don't get me wrong. But I don't mind baby steps."

"I do," she said. "I'm tired of being scared someone will find out."

Macy kissed her, then put her head on her shoulder. "Mind if I ask what brought on the change?"

"Guess the last couple of days were a wake-up call," she said. "Some things can't wait. Well, that and Earl, of all people. Pretty much told me no one cares, and to get my shit together."

"I always liked him," she said, smiling. "Remind me to get him a fruit basket."

"I think a bottle of bourbon would probably be more up his alley," she said, and they both laughed. "Don't suppose you know anyone qualified to be a dispatcher?"

"Don't tell me you fired him," she said, and Dana shook her head.

"Not even close," she said. "Made him our only detective."

"Smart move," she said. "He sure knows this town inside and out. I can probably come up with a name or two."

"I should get going," she said, making no move to get up. "Gotta help barricade Main street."

"See you there?" she said, and Dana nodded. "And don't worry. I won't molest you while you're on the job. Gotta respect the uniform, even if you look all manner of hot in it." Dana smiled and kissed her again, then stood up and put her hat on.

"Well, the criminal hordes are waiting," she said.

"Go get 'em," Macy said, smacking her on the butt as she left.

***

"Quiet crowd," Mayor Shelby said as they stood on the grand stand, watching as floats went by.

"I think everyone's still in shock," Dana said. "Honestly, I was a little surprised it wasn't canceled."

"People needed a distraction," he said. "Any news?"

"Waiting on the post-mortems for the official ruling," she said. "And there are a couple of questions I still need answered."

"Such as?" he said. "Far be it from me to tell you your business, but it would seem fairly cut and dried to me. It's a tragedy, but these were clearly suicides."

"Suspected suicides," she said. "There are some inconsistencies."

"Chief, I think it would be best for everyone if we could wrap this thing up and move on," he said. "It's natural to want to find some sort of explanation, some reason why this horrible tragedy happened, but dragging this out and chasing down ghosts that aren't there won't help anyone." He waved to several people on board the chamber of commerce float, smiling like the fool he was.

Dana smiled at a group of kids on the next float as they waved at her. "You're right about one thing, Mayor," she said, trying to keep her pleasant smile. "You're not even remotely qualified to tell me how to do my job."

"If the medical examiner rules that these deaths were suicides, then I expect that to be the end of it," he said. "And we both know that's exactly what they were. Tragic, preventable suicides."

"Especially by whoever built that platform," she said, letting it sink in. "Someone helped those kids do this."

"And the second group?" he said. "Or do you see some nefarious plot in that, too?"

"Suicides come in clusters," she said. "Ask any psychologist. But it seems like a damned strange way to do it, don't you think? Most people choose a way that's relatively painless. Some of those six kids lived for as long as three to five minutes."

She was saved his response when her phone vibrated. She stepped down and went behind the grandstand to take the call.

"Chief, it's Walt," he said as she answered. "Just finished up the autopsies on the hanging victims."

"That was fast," she said.

"Didn't seem right to make the families wait so I could catch the same parade I've seen for twenty years," he said. "Anyway, I don't think you're going to like it."

"You found something?" she said, walking to get away from the noise as the high school marching band went by.

"That's just it," he said. "There's not a goddamn thing here that even suggests any sort of foul play. They hung themselves, Chief. I can't see any reason to rule any other way."

"Okay," she said, taking a deep breath. "Anything on the cemetery victims?"

"Just getting ready to start," he said. "Got one on the table now. No defensive wounds, no odd bruising or anything else that suggests they were forced onto those stakes. It's gruesome as all hell, but I'm inclined to say the wound was self-inflicted. I'll be thorough, but I honestly don't think there's anything off here."

"Thanks, Walt," she said. She ended the call just as the phone vibrated again. It was Earl calling, and she answered on the second ring.

"Chief, I got someone you need to talk to," he said. "It's about that platform."

"Where are you?" she said.

"At the station," he said. "It'll be worth missing the parade, trust me."

"Ten minutes," she said. She started toward the station, trying not to be rude as people said hello. By the time she made it through the crowd, her patience was wearing thin, and she had to struggle not to take it out on the next person to slow her down.

She made it to the station with two minutes to spare. Earl stood up as she walked through the door. "Chief, this is Otis," he said as an older man wearing jeans and a t-shirt so white it had to be new stood up and held out his hand. He gave her a firm handshake, something she appreciated. She wasn't exactly tiny or delicate, but so many men seemed afraid they'd break her if they shook her hand.

"Morning," she said.

"Otis and I were just discussing carpentry," Earl said. "Otis is the best around."

"There's better out there," Otis said, and Dana nodded.

"Otis, tell the chief what you told me," Earl said, and Otis nodded quickly.

"I didn't build that thing," he said. "But a man does something long enough, he develops his own style. I've seen work like this before."

"I think I was just standing on it," she said, and he nodded.

"The grandstand," Otis said. "They been wheeling that old thing out for some fifteen years now."

"And do you know who built it?" she said. Earl nodded.

"Everyone knows who built it," Earl said. "Jack Anderson."

"I know that name," she said. "Where have I heard that?"

"He was killed some years ago in a fire," Earl said, staring at her as if to tell her to catch up already.

"Gavin Anderson's father," she said, and Otis nodded.

"Damned good carpenter, was old Jack," he said. "Even if he was a dirt-mean sonofabitch. You got that white two-story over on Elm, right?"

"Yes," Dana said.

"Well, Jack built your back deck," Otis said. "I helped him put it up. And if I didn't know no better, I'd swear old Jack built that damned platform."

"What can you tell me about Gavin?" she said.

"Good kid," Otis said, shrugging. "Poor boy, never really got over what happened to his daddy. There's folks that say he caused that fire, but that's a load of bull. Everybody who knew Jack would tell you he left those damn cigars of his burning in an ashtray more often than not when he was loaded, which was most nights."

"I understand Gavin had a hard time in school," Dana said, and Otis nodded.

"You know how kids can be," he said. "But he stuck it out for a long time."

"He dropped out of school, didn't he?" she said, and Otis shook his head.

"Not like you're thinking," he said. "He dropped out to get his GED. I don't know how much of that had to do with kids being mean, but he says it was just because he didn't want to spend another year there."

"What does he do now?" she asked, pretty sure she knew the answer.

"He works for me," Otis said. "Goes to school at night. He's one of my best guys, actually. Comes in early, stays late, busts his butt the whole time."

Dana nodded, standing up and shaking Otis's hand again. "Thank you," she said. "That's very helpful. Do you know where I could find Gavin?"

"He's out at the shop," Otis said. "I tried to get him to come see the parade, get out a little, but he don't like being around people. The scars, you know. He puts up a good show, but I think it bothers him more than he lets on. You don't think he had anything to do with those kids, do you?"

"Not really," Dana said. "Thank you for coming in, Otis."

Earl showed him out, then turned to face her. "You think that kid built the damned thing, don't you?"

"I think I need to talk to him," she said. "You disagree?"

"Not even a little," he said. "I dealt with Gavin a few times before I hung it up. Kid's got a lot of anger in him."

"Well then," she said. "You don't happen to know where Otis's shop is, do you?"

"I'd say so," he said, smiling. "It's half a mile from my house. Drank more beer in that shop than I care to remember."

CHAPTER TEN

"Gavin Anderson?" Dana said as they stepped inside the shop building. A young man stood with his back to them, marking up a two by four. She could see pink burn scars underneath his black ball cap, and she reminded herself not to flinch as he turned around.

The left side of his face was a mass of twisted scars. The left eye was clouded over, and the corner of his mouth had been pulled up in what she could only call a terrifying half-smile, exposing his teeth even with his mouth closed. He put a pencil behind his right ear, and it wasn't until then she noticed that most of his left ear was gone.

"Chief," he said. "Help you? We're technically closed right now, but I can take a message for Otis."

"Actually wanted a word with you, son," Earl said, and Dana nodded. Earl took the printouts of the platform pictures from his pocket and handed them to him.

"Looks like nice work," he said, flipping through them. "Gazebo?"

"Keep going," Earl said, and Gavin flipped through the pictures until he came to the wide angle shots that showed the whole structure.

"Shit," he said, almost dropping the pictures. "This is where those kids hung themselves, isn't it?"

"You don't happen to know who built that platform, do you?" Dana asked. He took a good look at it, then shook his head.

"Almost looks like Dad's work," he said. "Man was allergic to sloppy joints."

"Otis said the same thing," she said. "Where'd you learn carpentry?"

"About where you're thinking," he said. "From Dad, just like a few dozen other people. Dad taught a 4-H class for years."

"Any of these kids in those classes?" Dana said, handing him a list of the victims.

"No way," he said. "They were too young. I was the only real little kid he ever let touch a saw or a hammer. Guess he figured he could keep an eye on me easier."

"But you knew them," she said, and he nodded.

"Of course I did," he said. "I went to that school up until last year."

"Ever have any trouble with any of them?" she said, and he chuckled.

"Take a good look, Chief," he said, pointing to his face. "They go all the way down to my feet, if you're curious. Seventy percent coverage. Kids are assholes; it's kind of the default status. Yeah, they were pretty rough on me."

"That make you mad?" she said, and he shrugged.

"It was high school," he said. "No one enjoys high school. What is it you're working your way up to, Chief?"

"I need to know who built that platform," she said. "There's no way they didn't know what it was for."

"Actually, I'd bet they didn't have a clue," he said, picking up the pictures. "These are just copies, right?"

Earl nodded, and Gavin picked up a grease pencil from the bench. "Reason this looks like a gazebo is because it basically is," he said, making marks on one of the pictures before handing it over. "The platform itself is solid work. Nice, tight joints, straight cuts, no gaps or off angles. Look at the supports. They're slapped together at best."

"I'll be damned," Earl said, showing her what he was talking about. "Should have seen it."

"My guess? Whoever built this, they just built the gazebo," Gavin said. "Someone else jacked it up and put it on stilts. Not the easiest thing to do, but not impossible. What's this all about, anyway? I thought this was a suicide pact or something."

"Probably is," Dana said. "Just one last thing. Mind telling me where you were Thursday night, about midnight or so?"

"Sure," he said. "I was driving home from Springfield. I had class until ten. Stopped for a late dinner, was on the road home by eleven thirty. Didn't keep receipts or anything; didn't know I'd need an alibi."

"No one ever does," she said, and he smiled. She was a little ashamed of how much the sight of him smiling disturbed her. "Thanks for your time, Mr. Anderson." He shook hands with both of them, and they let him get back to work as they walked to the car.

"How'd that read to you?" she said as they stood at the car.

"Like a kid who's more or less got his shit together," he said. "You?"

"I think he's lying," she said after a minute. "I think he knows exactly who built that platform, because he built it himself."

"I don't see it," Earl said. "Kid like him, he's probably got a hell of a temper. He ain't gonna wait a year to get back at a bunch of kids picking on him."

"I don't know how he pulled it off yet," she said, "but he's a wrong guy. I know you see that."

"Kid's screwed up half a dozen ways," Earl said, nodding. "Hell, anyone in his shoes probably would be. But that don't add up to convincing twenty some kids to hang themselves in some crazy suicide pact. For that matter, how would he even do that?"

"I don't know," she said after a minute. "Maybe I'm looking for something that isn't there."

"Happens to the best of us," he said. "Spent a lot of time chasing down bullshit myself."

"What did you end up doing?" she asked.

"Chased it down anyway," he said, smiling. "I'm a stubborn old cuss."

****

They made it back to town as the parade was winding down. Poor Mark looked frazzled as he moved from one group of rowdy kids to a cluster of men drinking from a bottle in a brown paper bag. They got out of the car as he was politely trying to tell them there was no drinking in public.

"I'm afraid you're going to have to take it somewhere else," Mark said. "On foot."

"Free country," one of them said. "I pay my taxes. I can drink where I want."

"You heard him," Dana said. "Dump it or put it away."

"Scottie Dawson," Earl said, and the proud taxpayer almost snapped to attention. "You still got a case of the stupids, I see."

"Chief," he said, and Earl shook his head.

"That's her," he said, hooking his thumb at Dana. "And she told you to put it away. You'd be smart to listen; she ain't half as nice about it as I am."

Scottie twisted the lid on the bottle and dropped it in the trash. "Keys," Dana said, holding out her hand. All three of them handed over their keys. "You can pick them up at the station after you sober up. Go on."

They broke it up and wandered away. "Sorry, Chief," he said. "Didn't figure it'd be smart to make a scene just yet. Figured I could talk 'em out of it."

"I'll just wander around a bit," Earl said, giving her a nod.

"Polite is fine," Dana said. "Polite's a great way to start. But you're gonna have to learn when to stop being polite, Mark. Ask first, sure. But when asking doesn't work, you tell them. You're not a security guard, you're a police officer. Guys like that, they figure out pretty quick how far they can push you. Give them an inch, and you'll have no end of problems with them. You understand what I'm saying? Next time it might not be a nuisance charge. Next time it could be something serious, and that's how people get hurt."

"Yes ma'am," he said, looking properly chagrined.

"Come on, it's almost lunch time," she said.

"You want to take first?" he said, and she shook her head.

"Nah. I actually wanted to pick your brain a little," she said. "I'm sure the town will survive for an hour without us. Besides, word's out Earl has a badge again. I'd imagine most of the morons are busy hiding under their beds."

"You don't think he wants his old job back, do you?" he said, and she laughed.

"I think you'd have to beat him down pretty good to even make him think about it," she said. "But after this week, I might just give it to him."

✳✳✳

"Hey, Chief," Earl said as they walked into the station. "Just got off the phone with Brad out at the lumberyard. I'm on my way to go talk with him, see if he can tell me about how much lumber that platform would take."

"And if anyone's bought that amount lately," she said, nodding. "Call me if you get anything."

"Phones are forwarded to county," he said. "Talked to them this morning, they don't mind."

"Good," she said. It wouldn't work for long, but it would maybe give her time to find another dispatcher. City council would probably raise hell over adding another position, but she didn't care. Earl was too damned good at what he did to ride the phones all day.

After he was gone, she turned to Mark. "You grew up around here, right?" she said, and he nodded. "You remember a kid named Gavin Anderson?"

"Vaguely," he said. "I knew of him, of course, but I was a few years ahead of him. I'd graduated before he got to high school."

"What do you know about him?" she said, and he shrugged.

"Lost his dad in a house fire, got himself burned up pretty badly. Had a hard time of it in school. You know how kids are. You think he had something to do with all this?"

"I think he at least knows who built the platform," she said. "If he didn't do it himself."

"No crime in that," Mark said.

"There is if he knew why he was building it," she said.

"Mind if I speak freely?" he said carefully, and she shook her head.

"Not at all," she said.

"How sure are you this is about a crime, and not just about needing someone to be responsible?" he said. "Something like this happens, and we want someone to blame. We want to think someone must have done something, because it makes more sense than what happened."

She sat back in her chair. "Honestly, I don't know," she said. "Does seem pretty thin."

"Very thin," Mark said. "You talked to Walt this morning?"

"Yeah," she said. "And he says there's not a single thing to suggest it's anything but exactly what it looks like, a mass suicide by a bunch of confused kids."

"You know my dad, right?" he said, and she nodded.

"Used to be a doctor, didn't he?" she said, and he nodded.

"Now happily retired and driving my Mom crazy," he said with a grin. "Wanted me to be one, too. Even did two years of pre-med before I figured out I was the only one who didn't want me to be a doctor. Anyway, Dad loves to tell stories. One of his favorite is something they tell you first year of med school."

"Wash your hands?" she said, and he laughed.

"When you hear hoofbeats, think horses, not zebras," he said.

She let out a tired sigh. "Things are usually pretty much

exactly what they look like," she said.

"Guy gets shot in bed, you look at the wife," he said. "Car crosses three lanes of traffic and crashes without an explanation, driver's probably drunk."

"And when you find a group of kids hanging from nooses, chances are they put themselves there," she said, nodding. "There's just something wrong about it."

"There's all kinds of things wrong about it," he said. "I'm just not sure it adds up to a crime. If you want, we can run down the builder, but chances are it's just some guy making a buck. Odds are, we find him, and he tells us one of those kids paid him to build it."

"If that's the case, I'll let it go," she said. "But there's something about all this that doesn't sit right with me, and it's not just the platform. How the hell do twenty kids organize something like this, and no one knows about it?"

"Kids are better at keeping secrets than they get credit for," he said. "Not saying there probably weren't hints for someone to catch if they'd known to look, but it's not impossible. Maybe it is what it looks like."

"You're probably right," she said. "Meantime, humor me and see what you can dig up on Gavin Anderson." She gave him the details of his alibi for Thursday night.

"I'll get into it," he said, tossing his sandwich wrapper into the trash. He was headed for the parking lot when someone came bursting through the front door, yelling for her.

"Chief, you need to come quick! He's gonna jump!" She took a moment to see who was yelling. It was Chris St. John, and she knew there was trouble immediately. Chris was quite possibly the last person to ever panic for no reason.

"Who and where?" she said. "Show me." Mark followed her out the door.

"It's Henry MacNeil," he said. "He's up on the bank, and he looks like he means to jump."

CHAPTER ELEVEN

"I can get around back and get up on the roof if you can keep him talking," Mark said, and Dana nodded.

"Go," she said. "And be careful."

Mark nodded and took off running. She supposed it was possible MacNeil would see him, but it couldn't be helped. Earl came up to her as she started trying to get his attention.

"Henry," she called out. "Henry, it's Chief Atwater. Don't move, okay?" she said. "We'll get you down."

"You just stay back," Henry yelled. "I have to do this."

"No you don't, Hank," Earl said. "Now get down off there and let's talk about it."

"It's my fault," MacNeil said. "I could have stopped them, but I ignored it." He stepped up onto the ledge, wobbling slightly as a gust of wind caught him.

"Henry, don't move," Dana said.

"Kid trying to get around behind him?" Earl said quietly, and she nodded.

"There he is," she said. Mark approached MacNeil

carefully, moving slow so as not to spook him.

"Mr. MacNeil, it's Mark Sherman. You remember me?" he said as MacNeil turned quickly to face him.

"You just stay back," MacNeil said. "You can't help. I have to do this."

"No sir, you don't," Mark said, inching closer. "Sir, I'm not going to stand here and tell you I know what you're feeling, but this isn't the answer. I think you know that. Come on back over here, and we'll talk. Just you and me. We don't even have to come down off the roof yet, if you don't want. We can just talk." Mark inched closer to him, and Dana and Earl both saw it at the same time. Mark had a pair of handcuffs out behind his back.

"God damn it," Earl said quietly. "Don't be stupid, kid. You're too close. Get back."

"Mark, back off," Dana yelled, but he kept inching toward him, one hand held out.

"Please, Mr. MacNeil. Just come back over here, and we'll talk. Whatever's going on, I promise I'll listen."

"You can't help me," MacNeil said, shaking his head. "You don't understand. I could have stopped them. I could have made them stop, but I didn't. I let it happen, and now it's time to pay."

"God damn it, kid. Back off," Earl called out. MacNeil turned his attention to Earl, and Mark made his move. He grabbed MacNeil by the arm and cuffed his wrist. Dana saw everything happen in slow motion; Mark slapping the cuff on him, leaning forward to grab his shirt. MacNeil jerking his hand away, and losing his balance. Mark grabbing at him, trying to catch him as the momentum carried them both forward.

She watched in stunned horror as they both hit the pavement forty feet below. It seemed like forever before the first screams broke through the stunned silence.

"Jesus Christ," Earl said, snapping her out of it. He immediately started moving people back, barking orders and growling at people until they complied. Ordinarily she preferred a nicer approach, but right now Earl's way was getting it done, and that was all she cared about.

"What the hell?" someone said behind her, and she'd never wanted to hug someone more than she did Wendall at that moment. He stepped forward enough to see what had happened, and looked away. She had a brief moment to wonder if he was going to vomit, but he got it together.

"Everyone back," Earl barked as people tried to crowd in. "I said get back."

"Wendall," she said, her voice sounding incredibly hollow to her as Wendall nodded.

"I'll go grab some tape," he said, running for the station as she stepped forward and tried to help Earl control the crowd.

***

Two hours later, the crowd was safely contained behind the yellow crime scene tape, and the bodies were on their way to Walt's office. Wendall and Travis, who had come running the minute he heard someone was hurt, were busy taking witness statements down on the ground as she and Earl stood on the roof of the bank.

"The hell was he thinking?" she said, looking at the ledge. It was less than a foot wide, and the safety wall hit her about mid-thigh; perfect conditions to trip and fall, especially with someone pulling at you.

"He was thinking he could pull him in," Earl said. "He didn't know no better. You tried to tell him to back off. Hell, we both did."

"God damn it," she said, kicking the safety wall. "Of all the stupid fucking ways to die in this job."

"Ain't no good way to go," Earl said, shrugging. Dana nodded, forcing herself to get it together. She'd break down later. Right now she had a job to do.

"I need to call his parents," she said, taking a deep breath.

"I'll wrap this up," he said. "Go do what you need to do."

"Thank you, Earl," she said.

"Hell, don't thank me," he said, shaking his head. "I know I rode his butt pretty good, but I liked that boy. He

84

had this way of thinking around corners, you know? You could sit and watch him do it. I'm gonna miss that."

"Me too," she said, starting back toward the fire escape and climbing back down to the ground. She had a moment to gather herself before she made it around the building and had to go back to being the boss.

"Everyone saw it pretty much the same way," Travis said, flipping through his notebook. "Kid tried to grab him. MacNeil jerked away and fell, and he pulled Mark with him."

"I'm getting the same thing," Wendall said, looking a little pale as he stared at the large blood stain on the concrete. "Jesus, what a mess. How old was he, anyway?"

"Twenty-six," Dana said. "Would have been twenty-seven next month."

"Christ," Travis said, shaking his head.

"Earl's got the scene," she said. "I have to—I need to call his parents."

"I know his dad," Travis said. "Used to be my doctor. I can do it, if you want."

"No," she said, shaking her head as she patted him on the shoulder. "My department, my responsibility."

"What do you want me to do with them?" Travis said, looking over at a pair of city works department men. They were waiting for the go-ahead to clean up the blood.

"They're here already?" she said, surprised. "Takes them a week to even mark out a pothole, let alone fix it."

"I think someone's anxious to be rid of it," Travis said, looking off to her left, where Mayor Shelby was walking toward her.

Shit, she thought. She was tempted to just bail, but she knew better. Travis and Wendall would end up taking the majority of shit, at least until Earl came down and really made things ugly. "Chief," Shelby said, and she resisted the irrational urge to punch him. She could see herself doing it; burying a fist right in the center of his smug little face. Travis and Wendall must have seen it on her face, because they both stood by as he approached.

"Mr. Mayor, as I'm sure you're aware, we've got a lot going on right now," Travis said. "But I'm sure I can answer any questions you have."

"It's okay, Travis," she said, getting it together and putting a hand on his shoulder. "Mayor Shelby, I was just headed back to the station. You're welcome to walk with me, if you'd like."

"I just need to know if it's okay for the men to start cleaning up," he said quietly. "No disrespect for either man intended, but I'm worried about traumatizing anyone any further than they have been."

Dana took a deep breath, looking around the scene. Everything had been photographed, and she had dozens of witnesses, including herself and Earl, as to what had happened. She supposed there was no harm in releasing the scene.

"Go ahead," she said, and Mayor Shelby nodded to the two men, who started unloading a power washer from the back of their truck.

"I understand you promoted Earl Granby," he said, following her as she walked away. "I was under the impression he was retired."

"He's wasted as a dispatcher," she said. "And honestly, I can hire a dispatcher for a lot less than I can a detective."

"Certainly," he said. "Still, I think it would have been prudent to discuss the issue with me, first. Not everyone in town is a member of the Earl Granby fan club."

"I was under the impression personnel matters were under my authority," she said, stopping in the middle of the sidewalk. "Or was someone else appointed Chief while I was asleep last night?"

"No, of course not," he said. "Still, you have to admit Earl is a bit of a local figure. Not everyone has fond memories of his tenure as Chief."

"I'm sure there are all sorts of people who don't," she said. "Most of them are probably still in jail. He's a valuable resource, and it would be stupid not to take advantage of him as long as he's here. Now, if you're done second-guessing my hiring decisions, I have a notification to do."

"It is your department," he said, nodding. "Entirely your decision. He's your officer to deal with." She was tired, and probably in shock, but the message was loud and clear. Earl was her responsibility, and if he screwed up, she'd pay the price for it.

"Glad we understand each other," she said, shaking her head as she walked away from him. She climbed up the short flight of concrete stairs to the front door and let herself in, heading straight for the coffee pot.

She sat down at her desk, staring at the computer for a moment. She considered starting her report, but she knew better. She still needed Earl's statement, and the witness statements Travis and Wendall were gathering.

With no legitimate reason to stall any longer, she pulled Mark's personnel file and found the number she needed. She started to dial, but stopped. It was only an hour drive into Springfield, and this situation called for a face to face conversation.

It was going to be another long day, she thought as she dialed Earl's cell instead. "Earl, it's me. Think you can hold the fort for a few hours?"

"I reckon I can keep it in check," he said. "You headed to see his folks?"

"Can't really tell them something like this over the phone," she said, and she heard him grunt.

"I'll keep an eye on things," he said. "Go do what you gotta do. Might as well take the day."

"I can't do that," she said. "I still have to—I have to write the report."

"It ain't going nowhere," he said. "Me and the boys can handle things. But if it makes you feel better, I'll call if anything big breaks."

She supposed he was right; there wasn't much she could accomplish right now, especially with the way her head seemed to be wrapped in cotton.

CHAPTER TWELVE

Dr. Sherman was a handsome older version of his son, tall and broad-shouldered, with the touch of grey at his temples that gave him an air of distinguished authority. His wife Sarah seemed at first to be too young to have been Mark's mother, but up close Dana could see the faintest traces of her age. She had a moment to hope she aged half as well before they asked her to come inside and sit down.

She'd done more than her fair share of family notifications before, but this was the first time she'd had to do it for one of her officers. She'd found it best to be gentle but direct, or the family would try to find some loophole to question what she was telling them.

"Dr. Sherman, Mrs. Sherman," she said as they sat down in front of her. "I'm afraid there's no good way to say this."

"What's happened?" Mrs. Sherman said. "Is it Mark?"

"I'm afraid so," she said. "I'm sorry to tell you that Mark was killed this afternoon in the line of duty."

"What?" Dr. Sherman said. "No. That doesn't make any

sense. What happened?"

"He tried to intervene in a suicide attempt," she said. "He tried to pull the man back from a ledge. There was a brief scuffle, and Mark fell with him. I'm sorry," she said.

Mrs. Sherman started crying quietly, burying her head in her husband's shoulder as he comforted her the best he could.

She sat there for a moment in awkward silence as they tried to process what she'd just told them. After a moment, Dr. Sherman nodded. "When can—can we see him?"

"His body was taken to the medical examiner's office," she said. "He won't require a formal identification."

"Did," Dr. Sherman said, faltering for a moment. "Were you there? When it happened?"

"I was," she said, trying not to start crying herself. She'd done enough of that on the drive up. "There was nothing anyone could have done. It happened very fast."

Dr. Sherman nodded as Mrs. Sherman continued to sob. "When," he said, his breath catching for a moment. "When can we claim his body?"

She pulled one of Walt's cards from her pocket and slid it across the coffee table. "You can contact Dr. Howe's office at any time. He'll help you arrange all the details. Again, I'm very sorry for your loss."

"Thank you, Chief," he said, standing up to show her out. She made her escape, feeling about six inches high as she all but ran to the car and drove away before they could ask her any more questions.

She stopped for gas, annoyed that her fleet fuel card wasn't accepted at the station closest to her. She paid for it out of her own pocket, not even remotely convinced that she'd ever be reimbursed for it. It would have normally pissed her off, but right now she didn't really care. She had been here on official business, but it was really a personal trip; she could have just as easily called.

***

The drive back to town seemed to take forever, and by

89

the time she pulled into her driveway, the sun was down. She let herself in the front door, and was almost immediately greeted by Macy, who made her sit down on the couch and brought her a cup of coffee.

"You know, you don't have to park in back any more," she said, but Macy shushed her as she sat down beside her.

"Doesn't matter right now," she said as Dana leaned into her. "I heard what happened. Hell, I think the whole town heard. How are you holding up?"

"I'm not sure yet," she said, closing her eyes as Macy massaged her shoulders. "I just notified his parents. Lovely couple."

"I'm so sorry," she said, kissing the top of her head. "He seemed like a nice guy."

"He was," Dana said. "Sometimes a little too nice, but a good kid. That feels good," she said as Macy continued to work at the knot that had been growing between her shoulder blades since yesterday.

"Kind of the point," she said, and Dana smiled.

"I never asked how the rest of your meeting went," she said.

"Well, I didn't get fired, if that's what you mean," she said. "Pretty sure I didn't make any friends on the school board, though."

"How are you holding up?" Dana said, sitting up. "You knew Henry."

"Still in shock, I guess," she said. "Never would have thought he'd do something like that."

"The doctors call it contagion," Dana said. "Read all about it last night. One person commits suicide, others get the idea. Especially if they're feeling guilt over it."

"He was," she said. "We talked about it last night. He was being pretty hard on himself for not seeing the signs. I tried to tell him none of us saw it. I thought I got through to him."

"What happened to those kids wasn't his fault," Dana said. "They did what they did. They planned and organized it. And what he did isn't your fault, either."

"I know," Macy said, looking sad. "Doesn't really help,

though."

"Didn't imagine it would," she said. They sat quietly for a minute before she spoke again. "I let him go up there. I knew he'd never worked a jumper before, didn't know the rules. But I let him go up."

"He was doing his job," she said, stroking her arm.

"I could have told him to stay put, gone up myself," she said. "But I kept telling myself he'll never learn if I don't let him do things. So stupid," she said. Before she knew it was coming, she broke down and cried as Macy held her.

"He was just a fucking kid," she said, shaking her head. "Just a stupid, green fucking kid that didn't know his ass from his elbow. I let him go up on that roof, and now he'll never learn. He'll never," she said, unable to continue.

"It's okay," Macy said, holding her as she finally let go.

"I just," Dana said. "I can't get it out of my head. I keep hearing it, over and over. I keep hearing him hit the sidewalk, like someone had chucked a goddamn watermelon off the roof. God, I can still hear it."

"Shh," Macy said. "It's okay. Let it go."

Unable to hold it off any longer, Dana finally let herself break down and cried as Macy held her, rocking her back and forth.

Eventually she was done, and Macy led her into the kitchen, where of course she'd cooked dinner. She was surprised to find she was actually hungry, and ate with quiet enjoyment.

After dinner, they did the dishes together. Dana dried as she listened to Macy talk. Not about anything heavy or sad; she just talked, letting Dana ride along with her thoughts to avoid her own, which were turning inward and dark in a way she didn't like. Macy always rambled when she was doing something, and even though Dana usually enjoyed listening to her as she talked, tonight she didn't just want to hear it. She needed to hear her talking; it reminded her there were things in her world besides death and loss.

When her phone vibrated in her pocket, she almost ignored it. Responsibility won out over selfishness, though, and she answered it before it could go to voicemail.

"Chief Atwater," she said, answering without reading the caller ID.

"It's Earl," he said. "Didn't want to bother you at home, but I thought you'd want to hear this."

"Go ahead," she said, sitting down.

"Talked to Ed Hackney a little bit ago," he said. "He says he sold just a bit over the right amount of grade one timbers to a fellow a week ago. Care to guess who signed for the order?"

"Gavin Anderson," she said, and he clucked his tongue.

"Right in one," he said. "Figured I should check in with you before I go any further."

"Pick him up," Dana said. "I'll be in the station in twenty minutes." She put the phone away and started to explain, but Macy cut her off with a surprise kiss.

"Go," she said. "Take care of whatever it is. I'll be here when you get back."

"You're entirely too good for me," Dana said, and Macy smiled.

"Well, duh," she said. "Now go catch bad guys. You know how hot it makes me when you arrest people."

"Tease," she said, giving her another kiss.

CHAPTER THIRTEEN

"Chief," Wendall said as she came into the station. "Earl just called in, said he's on his way in with Gavin Anderson."

"Good," she said. They didn't actually have an interrogation room, so she'd have to do the interview in her office.

"You talk to his folks?" Wendall said carefully, and she nodded.

"Nice people," she said. "Guess that shouldn't be much of a surprise."

"Doesn't seem right," Wendall said. "If it had been some skel on a traffic stop, or maybe if he'd walked in on a domestic," he said, letting the thought trail off.

"There'd be someone to punish," she said, nodding. "I know."

"Wouldn't make it any easier, I guess," he said. "But at least it'd make some kind of damn sense."

"I shouldn't have let him go up," she said. "He'd never worked a jumper before. Didn't have a damn clue what he was doing."

"Beg pardon, Chief, but that's just bullshit," he said, surprising her. "They teach that at the academy, you know. He knew the rules. As for the rest, he was never going to get the experience if we did it for him. Wasn't your fault. Wasn't his, either. It was an accident, that's all."

"I know," she said, adjusting her desk blotter. She was saved from her own introspection when Earl came through the back door, leading a handcuffed Gavin Anderson inside.

"This is bullshit," Anderson said as Earl led him to the cage. "What am I being arrested for, buying lumber? I'm a freaking carpenter, genius."

"Sit down and shut up," Earl said, making her cringe slightly as he opened the cell and turned him around, taking the cuffs off and closing the door on his way out.

"Chief, this is stupid," he said as she came out. She'd intended to talk to him in her office, but now that Earl had tossed him in a cell, it would look like she was undermining his authority if she let him out.

"We need to have a conversation, Mr. Anderson," she said. "And this time I think you'd be smart to tell me the truth. You bought a load of grade one timbers from the lumberyard last week," she said. "Ed Hackney tells me that's exactly what was used to build the platform those kids hung themselves from."

"I build things for a living, Chief," he said.

"You do the buying for Otis now?" Earl said. "Because last I knew, he didn't trust his own damned kids to do that."

"I do a little side work now and then," he said.

"I imagine so," Dana said, holding up a picture of the platform. "I'm going to ask you again, Gavin. You built this, didn't you? You built it, knowing damn well what those kids meant to do. That makes it a crime. Tell me who asked you to build it."

"No one," he said, "because I didn't build the damned thing."

"You know what I think?" Wendall said, surprising them all. He usually didn't sit in on interrogations, not that there were many to sit in on these days. "I think you got word of what was coming. I think you found out the same group of kids who made your life sheer hell for years were going to do this horrible thing, and you saw a chance to get even. I bet you didn't even charge them, did you?"

"That how it happened, Gavin?" she said.

"Even assuming I built something for one of them, which I didn't, what's the crime?" Gavin said. "Can't blame a guy for filling a customer order."

"If you knew what they were going to do, and you built the platform for them to do it, that's assisting a suicide," Dana said. "Five years, minimum. If you built this thing and didn't know, what's the harm in telling me the truth, son?"

"Because I'm sitting in a cell?" he said. "You want the truth? Fine. I spent a lot of years hating those fucks. Too many years. It wasn't doing a damned thing to them, but it was eating me alive. I got help. Learned to let it go. I'm not exactly busted up they're gone, but I wouldn't help them kill themselves. They shouldn't have gotten off that easy. I wanted them to live with the things they did."

"And the second group?" Dana asked. "You hate any of them, too?"

"Don't even know who they were," he said. Dana showed him the list of names.

"Most of them were pretty cool," he said. "We didn't exactly hang out together, but they didn't screw with me. Not like Chase or the others."

"Help me understand," Dana said. "I can't imagine hating someone as much as you say over a little teasing."

"A litte teasing," Gavin said, chuckling. It made the distorted corner of his mouth move. "You want to know what they called a little teasing?" He pulled up his shirt and turned around. The scar tissue was broken up by new wounds that looked to be just a couple of years old.

"Chase and his buddies decided they'd help me out," he said. "Three of them tackled me behind the wood shop and held me down while he sanded my back. Said he was just taking away the scars for me. Said I should thank him. And in case you're wondering, yes, it hurt like a motherfucker. But the infection was what really screwed me over. Missed enough school I was going to have to repeat my senior year, again. That's when I said fuck it and dropped out."

"You never reported it," Dana said, and he laughed.

"Yeah, because I'm sure that would have gone over well," he said. "Like I don't catch enough shit walking down the street without getting most of the starting basketball team arrested. But that was just the last in a long line of shit. You know what it's like to have half your skin so tight you can't move well enough to even dress out for gym class? How many lumps of charcoal I found in my locker? You know what my favorite was? Coming out of class to find my locker on fire. That was always a blast."

"No one reported any fires at the school," Dana said. "Especially arson."

"Yeah, well, they wouldn't, would they? Not with a winning basketball team to protect. The boosters love the jocks, and the boosters bring in the money. What's one crispy critter freak compared to the new gym floor?"

"You're telling me school officials covered all that up?" Dana said.

"I'm telling you they told me right to my face to quit being so 'sensitive.' MacNeil, the guy who swan dived off the bank today? Pulled me out of the hall one day about a week after the belt sander thing, told me I needed to think hard about what had happened. Said if I did that, I'd realize it was just an accident, and they were just trying to help me get to the nurse. Those bastards damn near killed me, more times than I care to count. You know, this isn't even from the original fire?" he said, holding up his right hand to show them a section of scar tissue on his palm in a straight line about a quarter inch wide.

"That what I think it is?" Earl said, and he nodded.

"Heated up a screwdriver and pressed it into my hand," he said. "That was freshman year. They were just getting warmed up. So, you still think I hated them over a few names and some laughing?"

Dana looked him over for a minute. "I think you had plenty of reason to want them dead," she said.

"And if they'd been stabbed or shot in the face, I'd

understand you wanting to talk to me," he said. "Hell, I'd suspect me, too. But they killed themselves, Chief. I'd like to think it was because they finally realized what rotten shitheads they were, but honestly? I think they just wanted attention. Now, unless you're actually going to charge me with something you can prove, I'd like to go. I've got homework to do."

Dana walked away from the cage, stepping into her office. Earl and Wendall followed her. "Thoughts?" she said as Wendall closed the door.

"I think he's had himself a pretty good hate boiling for a lot of years now," Earl said. "Something like that festers, when it breaks out, it ain't exactly neat and tidy."

"He's screwed up, no doubt about that," Wendall said. "But honestly, I think he's got a right to be. Sounds to me like they were trying to kill him. I'll tell you what's bugging me more than him."

"The school," she said, and Wendall nodded.

"If half of what he says is true, then I don't see how we look away from it," Wendall said.

"Basketball's always been king around here," Earl said. "Ain't gonna lie, I let a few of them slide over the years for the sake of the team. Nothing big, mind you. But I'd catch 'em drinking, maybe bending the speed limit a little bit now and then."

"Go along to get along," Dana said, nodding. She wasn't some naive idealist; she knew how things worked. For some people, the rules were just a little different. "But kids sneaking beer or drag racing is a pretty damned far cry from assault and battery. Hell, some of it sounds like it could have been charged with attempted murder."

"Them fires are bugging me a little," Earl said. "Like I said, I might have let a little small-time shit slide, but I'd have been up someone's ass to the shoulders over that."

"What should we do with him?" Wendall said, looking out at the cage. Gavin had sat down on the cot and was currently leaning his head back, his eyes closed.

"Cut him loose," Dana said. "End of the day, he's right. We can't prove he built anything, and even if we could, we've got nothing to prove he knew what they were planning. We've got other things to worry about right now."

Wendall went to let Gavin out, and Earl closed the door behind him. "This the part where you tell me there might have been a better way to go about that?" he said, and she shrugged.

"Normally, yeah," she said. "But right now I couldn't care less. You knew Henry MacNeil, right?"

"Since we were kids," Earl said, nodding. "Played ball together."

"That sound like something he'd do?" she said. "Cover up something that big to protect the basketball team?"

"I'd like to tell you no way in hell," Earl said, sitting down. "But honestly? Yeah, I can see him making it go away. If not to protect the team, then to protect the school itself."

Dana nodded. "He wouldn't be the only one in on it," she said. "Not something that big."

"Depends on how far the kid pushed it," he said. "A little 'boys will be boys,' a little 'where's your school spirit' and 'don't be such a baby,' and maybe he finally gets the message it don't matter."

"Maybe," she said. "And maybe he's just yanking our chains. Maybe it wasn't as bad as he said."

"I don't know much," he said. "End of the day, I'm really nothing but a grunt. But I'll tell you this much. If that kid was lying, then he's the best damned liar I've ever seen, because I believe him."

"So do I," Dana said. "Which just begs the question. What do we do about it?"

"Ain't much we can do about what happened to him," Earl said. "According to him, most of them responsible are already gone. But sounds to me like maybe it's time for someone to take a hard look at that school."

"Have to wait until Monday," she said, and he nodded.

"I'll hang out until Travis comes on," he said. "Go get some rest."

"No arguments here," she said, and he laughed.

"That'd be a first," he said.

CHAPTER FOURTEEN

True to her word, Macy was waiting for her when she came home. She stopped at the closet to put her gun away and hang up her duty belt before collapsing next to her on the couch.

"Big crime wave?" Macy said, and Dana shook her head.

"Probably a dead end," she said. She stretched out on the couch, her head in Macy's lap as she started a movie on Netflix. "Came across something else, though. Might be big. Like real trouble big."

"Sounds promising," she said. "Wanna tell me about it?"

"I was actually hoping I could ask you about it," she said. "You've been teaching there what, like six years now?"

"About that," she said. "What's on your mind?"

"You remember me asking about a kid named Gavin Anderson?" she said.

"I do," she said. "Bright as hell. Sad story, though."

"Yeah, the fire," she said. "He told me a hell of a story tonight, and I gotta wonder how much of it is true. You ever see him being bullied?"

"Too often," she said. "I tried to step in, but he wouldn't talk to me. Said it would just make it worse."

"How bad did it get?" Dana asked as Macy began playing with her hair.

"Pretty bad," she admitted.

"Like assault bad? Arson bad?" she asked, and Macy looked uncomfortable.

"I never saw it," she said. "Not directly, mind you. But it's impossible not to hear things."

"Gavin says Chase Garner and some of his buddies held him down and took a belt sander to his back," Dana said. "Said they told him they were trying to help him with the scars. Missed a bunch of school over it."

"I remember him missing school," she said. "All we were told was that it was medical issues. Jesus, a belt sander?"

"Looked like it to me," she said. "Earl believed him, anyway. Said the infection almost killed him. There was a lot more. Put a hot screwdriver in his good hand, set his locker on fire."

"Like I said, I never saw anything directly," Macy said. "You know I would have raised hell." Dana patted her leg and nodded.

"Here's the tough question," Dana said, sitting up. "Don't shoot me for asking. Do you think Henry MacNeil or anyone else might have swept it under the rug to protect the basketball team?"

"I'd like to think not," Macy said after a minute. "But everyone knows the basketball team is the ruling class around here. Word has it anything below a C average, and you're 'highly encouraged' to look at it again. And Henry was all about the basketball team, let me tell you. So yeah, much as it might suck, I don't have a hard time believing they'd soft-pedal something to keep the team going."

She curled up next to her, lost in her own thoughts. "I might be about to step on a whole shoe store's worth of toes here," she said. "Could get ugly. For me and anyone near me."

"Screw it," Macy said. "If they did bury this kind of

thing, then they broke the law. Besides, it's about time someone upset the apple cart a little."

"Just thought you should know what you're getting yourself into here," Dana said. "Especially since I made it damn near impossible for you to deny any involvement with me last night."

"I'm not afraid of a little hardball," Macy said. "People like that, they don't know what to do with someone who isn't afraid of them. Personally, I'm looking forward to seeing some people sweat."

"Any idea where to start?" she said, and Macy nodded.

"I might be able to point you in the right direction," she said. "I'd start with Melody."

"Hagerrman? The counselor?" she said, and Macy nodded.

"She sees a hell of a lot more than anyone thinks," she said. "And she's not a fan of the privilege system, that's for sure."

"You think she knew what was happening to Gavin?" she asked, and Macy shrugged.

"I can't say what she knew or didn't know," she said. "But if I were going to ask about it, she's where I'd start."

****

"Tell me you at least went home," Dana said as she walked into the station, where Earl was already at his desk.

"Sure I did," he said. "Showered, grabbed something to eat. Even took a little catnap in my rocker."

"Didn't someone who looks a hell of a lot like you just give me a big speech about not burning myself out?" she said, and he smiled.

"I'm an old man," he said. "I've done my share of sleeping."

She almost asked if Mark was on yet, and bit her tongue. "I had something I wanted to run by you," she said, and he nodded as she sat down.

"Bet we're thinking the same thing," he said. "We're fixing to crap in a whole lot of cereal bowls, aren't we?"

101

"You are a poet," she said, smiling. "But yeah, I think so. If anyone at the school covered up for what that kid says happened, then they were complicit in the crime. Accessory after the fact. I asked the DA on the way in."

"And what did that rotten old bitch have to say?" he said, and she smiled. Earl's wars with the district attorney were the stuff of legend; rumor had it they'd been an item once, which was the only way to explain why they hated each other so much.

"She said go slow, be careful, but get into it," she said. "Basically she's covering her ass. If there's really something there, she doesn't want to look like she tried to quash it. And if there's not, she doesn't want to look like she was part of a witch hunt."

"Sounds about right," he said. "Well, 'slow' and 'careful' ain't never really been part of my style."

"Which is why I need you to go talk to Gavin Anderson again. Just talk," she cautioned him quickly. "We need names of anyone who might have seen anything they did to him. The assaults, the arsons, any of it."

"I take it we believe him, then," Earl said, and she nodded.

"I don't think there was much question about that," she said. "You saw the marks on his back. That look like a belt sander to you?"

"It did," Earl said. "And that burn on his hand. I seen something like it before. He didn't get that in no fire, I'll guarantee that."

"Okay then," Dana said, standing up. "Find me a witness. And Earl? Let's make sure he understands we're trying to help him, okay? Try not to smack him around if you don't have to."

"I don't always slap people around," he said, and she shook her head. "Well, not everyone. Where you headed?"

"Guess I'll go see if I can't step on some toes," she said.

***

Dana parked the cruiser in the visitor parking lot and

walked through the front door, drawing attention from students on their way to class. She had to smile a little at how nervous some of them seemed, and she wondered idly what sort of goodies she'd find if she did a random locker check. "Not today, kids," she said to herself as she headed for the office. "I'm after bigger game."

She was surprised at how pissed she was, but somewhere on the short drive between the station and the school, it had started bubbling up. She reminded herself to keep it in check as she walked down the hall, stopping when her phone vibrated.

"Chief, I'm out here at Gavin Anderson's place," Earl said. "He gave me a name, Brian Calhoun. He's a junior now."

"Good work, Earl," she said. "I'm headed in to see the principal now."

"Good luck," Earl said. "He's a cranky old bastard. You want me to meet you there?"

"I can handle him," she said. "Think you could swing by Walt's and pick up those autopsy reports?"

"Sure," he said. "Call me if that ornery old cuss gives you any grief."

"Will do," she said, shaking her head as she put the phone away. She had a witness; now she just needed to find him.

"Morning, Dolores," she said as she approached the main desk.

"Morning, Chief," she said with a smile. Dolores had been the secretary here as long as anyone could remember. "What can I do for you?"

"I need to talk to one of your students," she said. "Brian Calhoun."

"Let's see," she said, typing. "Oh, yes. He's in Miss Macy's History class. Just down the hall, second door on the right." Dolores gave her a prim little smile that said she knew perfectly well Dana knew right where it was.

"Thanks, Dolores," she said. She made good her escape before the nice old lady could offer her condolences on Mark; it was a little more than she could stomach at the moment.

She walked down the hall, nodding to a few students with hall passes in their hands. She saw Macy's door open just ahead, and she could hear her lecturing.

"Okay, so who can tell me what Operation Market Garden was, and why it was important?" Macy said as she stood just outside the door. She smiled as no one answered. "Come on, people, this was in the reading. Market Garden, anyone. No one?"

"Operation Market Garden was an attempt to punch through into the heart of Germany, and hopefully end the war by Christmas of '44," Dana said. "And it was important mostly because it failed."

"Thank you," Macy said. "Good to know someone's read a book around here. What can we do for you, Chief?"

"I need to speak with Mr. Calhoun," she said, and a kid stood up.

"Am I in some kind of trouble?" he asked, and Dana shook her head with what she hoped was a friendly smile.

"No, not at all," she said. "Just a couple questions." He grabbed his things and followed her out into the hall.

"What's the problem?" he said, sounding wary.

"You know Gavin Anderson?" she asked, and he nodded.

"Yeah," he said. "Good guy."

"So you two hang out a lot?" she asked.

"Used to," he said. "He works a lot now. Still see him now and then, you know. Why?"

"I understand Gavin had a rough time of it here," she said. "Think you could tell me about that?"

"I take it you don't mean the usual bullshit—I mean, the usual stuff," he said, and she nodded. "I was there when Chase and his buddies jumped him with the sander. I tried to stop it, but someone sucker-punched me. I woke up, and Gavin was bleeding all over the place."

"Did you tell anyone?" she said. "Someone from the school?"

"I tried," he said, shaking his head. "They made it real clear I must have made a mistake."

"Brian, this is important," she said. "Who did you tell, and were you very clear about what you saw?"

"Hell, I told everyone," he said. "The guidance counselor, the vice principal, even the principal and superintendent. They blew me off. I wanted to go to the cops, but Gavin said they wouldn't believe me, anyway."

"I believe you, Brian. Would you be willing to sign a statement about what you just told me?"

"Hell yes," he said. "You know, since they killed themselves, everyone's been walking around this place acting like Chase and his buddies were freaking saints. About time someone told the truth."

"Good man," she said, clapping him on the shoulder. "Feel like cutting class to do your civic duty?"

"Even better," he said, smiling.

CHAPTER FIFTEEN

She dropped Brian back off at the front door, then went to park the car so he had plenty of time to get to class without being seen with her any more than necessary. He'd put a lot on the line for her just now; no point in making life any harder for him.

"Principal Mather in?" she said as she walked past the front desk.

"I'm afraid he's in a meeting," Dolores said. "I'd be happy to grab you a cup of—Chief, I'm sorry, but he's busy at the moment."

Dana ignored her and walked into his office. If someone had called central casting and asked for a hard-assed principal, they would have probably sent Carl Mather. He was something of a legend in town; obviously cut from the same cloth as Earl, he was known to wade into fistfights and snatch both offenders up by the collars to drag them bodily to the office. He looked up at her as she stepped into the office, staring her down. She gave it right back to him; she wasn't a high school kid he could shut down with a glare.

There was a man sitting across from his desk, looking nervous as they stared each other down. Easy, she told herself. No reason to come at him hard just yet.

"I apologize for barging in," she said. "But I'm afraid there's a very sensitive matter we need to discuss that really can't wait, concerning some of your students."

"Of course," he said. "Joel, could we pick this up later?"

"Sure," Joel said, standing up. "Chief," he said, almost managing not to stare at her tits on the way out. She waited until he was gone before sitting down.

"I hope there's a very good explanation for this, Chief," he said. "I don't imagine I need to tell you things are in a bit of an uproar around here at the moment."

"No," she said. "And I wouldn't be taking up your time if it weren't important. But when I receive a report of a crime, I'm required to investigate it."

"A crime?" he said. "I'm sorry, I assumed you were here about—about what happened."

"It's related," she said. "What can you tell me about Gavin Anderson?"

"Gavin Anderson," he said, nodding. "Basically a good kid, but he had more than his share of problems. No small wonder, with all he went through. Has he done something?"

"Mr. Anderson is the victim," she said. "You're required to keep records of any and all reported incidents, aren't you?"

"We are, and we do. But I'm afraid you may not have the whole picture concerning Gavin. As I said, the poor boy has a lot of emotional problems. Sometimes he didn't always see things the way they actually happened."

"You're saying he lied about an assault that happened on school grounds last year?" she said.

"He was mistaken," Mather said, shaking his head. "He tripped and fell on a piece of equipment and injured himself. A few students tried to help him, but he lashed out at them. Broke one poor boy's nose, in fact."

"I probably would have broken a lot more than that if someone had held me down and taken a belt sander to me," she said. "I need to see those records, Mr. Mather."

"I'm afraid there are no records, Chief," he said. "Once Mr. Anderson had time to think about what had happened, he changed his mind. He apologized to the boy whose nose he broke, and that was the end of it."

She nodded and stood up. "I'm afraid you're not fully grasping the seriousness of this situation, Mr. Mather. I have witnesses who are willing to testify you and other members of this administration have actively discouraged victims and witnesses of criminal activity from reporting or pursuing the matter. You are aware, of course, that intimidating a witness is a crime, sir?"

"That sounds a lot like an accusation, Chief," he said. He reached into his desk and pulled out a card, sliding it across to her. "I believe any further discussion should take place through the district's lawyers."

"This isn't going away, Mr. Mather," she said, picking up the card. "I think you'll find I'm a lot harder to intimidate than a couple of high school kids, or someone who works for you."

"Good day, Chief," he said, picking up his pen. "I'm sure you can find your way out."

Dana nodded and left, thinking that if he wasn't on the phone with his boss in the next thirty seconds, she'd eat his desk.

***

"Slimy little peckerwood," Earl said after she'd finished filling him in on her conversation with Mather. "We got the Calhoun boy's statement. Think that's enough to get us in the door again?"

"It's a start," she said. "Be nice if we had someone else to add to it."

"I don't reckon that's gonna be a problem," Earl said with a grin as the front doors opened. She turned to see Macy standing in front of a half-dozen teachers, all of whom looked angry enough to slap a bear.

"You do that?" she said quietly, and Earl grinned.

"And they say I was never any good at reaching out to the

108

public.”

“I take it you're in need of witness statements,” Macy said, and Dana smiled. “We've all had the administration threaten to fire us if we didn't change grades or ignore fights.”

“Well then,” Dana said. “Let's get your statements.”

“Right this way, Miss Macy,” Earl said, and Dana nodded. Best to make sure everything was by the book on this one.

She motioned for everyone else to have a seat, and led a woman she recognized as the art teacher back to her office. “Have a seat, please,” she said, and the woman sat down.

“My name is Tina Gleason,” she said. “I'm the art teacher at the high school.”

Dana grabbed an interview form and started taking notes. “Okay,” she said. “What is it you saw?”

“I caught two boys setting a locker on fire,” she said. “I dragged them down to the office, and I was about to call the police when Henry stopped me.”

“Henry MacNeil, the vice principal?” she said, and Gleason nodded.

“Told me I must have been mistaken,” she said, shaking her head. “I don't like to speak ill of the dead, Chief, but he shut me down like that.” She snapped her fingers for emphasis. “Soon as he saw who the boys were, it was over. No suspension, no police report, nothing. They ended up missing sixth period to run laps, and that was the end of it.”

“Who were they?” she asked. “The boys who lit the fire?”

“Chase Garner and Clint Cooper,” she said.

“And you're certain they were starting a fire?” she said. “There's no possible way you were mistaken at all?”

“They dumped a bottle of lighter fluid inside and struck the match,” she said. “I know what I saw.”

“Okay,” Dana said. “You witnessed Chase Garner and Clint Cooper setting an intentional fire. You brought them to the office and attempted to notify the police, but were prevented from doing so at the time by Henry MacNeil, Vice Principal.”

“That's correct,” she said.

"Did Mr. MacNeil threaten or in any way coerce you into complying?" she asked. "Did he state or imply any sort of negative consequences for not complying?"

"He 'explained' to me that the basketball team brings in money from the boosters club," she said. "He told me all about how that money pays for a lot of things, including the art department, and wouldn't it be a terrible shame if suddenly we couldn't buy supplies or materials?"

"Got it," Dana said. "Do me a favor and read over that, make sure I got it all down right. Here's a pen in case you need to make any corrections. I'll be right back." She stepped out of the office and waved Earl over as he was finishing up Macy's statement.

"I've got one saying MacNeil threatened her department's funding if she didn't play ball," she said. "That's coercion."

"Same here," he said. "Said Mather told her that everyone goes along to get along, and those that don't, don't make it very long."

"Son of a bitch," she said. "She never told me that."

"Probably 'cause of that look on your face right about now," he said, and she nodded. "Don't get me wrong, I've been about half-way ready to kick his ass for twenty years. But much as I'd like to do it my way, I think we'd be smart to do it yours this time."

"Okay," she said. "Get their statements. Make damned sure they were specifically threatened or coerced in some way." Earl nodded, looking back at the other people waiting patiently in the lobby.

"Where you headed?" he said.

"I'm going to go annoy the shit out of the DA until she gives me an arrest warrant," she said, and he smiled.

"Probably better you than me," he said. "Doubt she'd throw a stapler at you."

"A stapler?" she said, shaking her head. "What in the world did you do to that woman?"

"No ma'am," he said, laughing. "That's a long and winding road we ain't got time to go down."

Macy stopped her on the way out, and they stepped off to one side to speak quietly. "You never told me Mather threatened to fire you," she said.

"And do you tell me every time some idiot threatens you?" she said with a smile. Dana just shook her head. "I figured it was just hot air."

"What did you see?" she said.

"Clint Cooper and a couple of other guys shoved a freshman into his locker and slammed the door," she said.

"Sounds familiar," she said.

"Just typical pranks, unless the kid doesn't fit and he ends up with three broken ribs and a severe cut on his back from the latch," she said, and Dana gasped. "I gave Earl his name."

"We'll run it down," she said.

"Where are you headed?" Macy said, and Dana couldn't resist smiling.

"Off to see Earl's old girlfriend," she said.

"Not done stirring the pot yet?" she said, and Dana shook her head.

"I'm just getting started," she said.

The DA's office was in City Hall just down the street; it seemed silly to drive less than a block, but she and Earl were the only ones on duty. She needed to be able to respond to a call if one came in.

She checked in with the secretary and was told to go right in; apparently she'd come at a good time. Helen Sharpe was a short, severe-looking woman with short, gray hair who constantly looked like she'd just bitten into a lemon. "Chief," she said, shuffling files on her desk. "To what do I owe the pleasure?"

"I have at least three signed affidavits saying administrators at the school threatened or coerced witnesses into not reporting criminal activity," she said. "My officer is taking more statements to that effect as we speak."

"And this is solid?" she said. "These people came in of their own accord?"

"We contacted several individuals who would have been in a position to witness the incidents, pursuant to a complaint from a victim," she said. Helen nodded. "They each independently stated that either the principal or the vice principal coerced them into not filing a police report. We have names of other victims that we'll be contacting shortly. I fully expect them to corroborate."

"I take it you made contact with the principal this morning," she said, and Dana nodded.

"I asked him if there had been any reported assaults or arsons as stated by the complainant," she said. "He gave me what I believe to be a false statement, saying that there were no such records."

"I received a call from an attorney for the school district an hour ago," she said. "According to him, you shoved your way into his office and accused him of covering up a crime."

Dana stopped for a moment, then nodded. "That's fair," she said, and Helen smiled.

"How sure are you about this, Chief?" she said. "Because this is just the sort of thing that ruins careers, for everyone involved, if it's not solid."

"I'm ready to arrest him right now," she said. "The fact it's so sensitive is the only reason I'm here instead of asking Judge Turner for a warrant."

Helen nodded. "Pick him up," she said. "Obstruction of justice and witness tampering. And Chief Atwater?"

"Yes ma'am?" she said, stopping at the door.

"Tell Earl I said hello," she said, and Dana smiled.

"I'll do that," she said.

CHAPTER SIXTEEN

"Chief," Earl said as she stepped inside. The last of the teachers was just leaving as she walked over to him. "I got three more names out of it."

"We'll run them down," she said, holding up the warrant. "After we pick up Mather. You want to come along?"

"Hell, I'll drive," he said, smiling.

They pulled into the high school a few minutes later. It had taken a little doing to convince Earl he didn't need to use the lights or siren; apparently he'd been just waiting for an excuse to arrest Mather on something. She was mildly concerned he apparently kept all his grudges neatly organized and filed, but now wasn't the time.

"Let me do the talking," she said as they got out of the car. "I'd like to take him in without fighting him, if possible."

"Sure, spoil my fun," Earl said, and she had to just shake her head and try not to laugh. The old man was every bit as full of piss and vinegar as the greenest rookie she'd ever met.

The only real problem was that he had enough experience to know better. It was just one more thing in a laundry list of concerns she had about having him back on the street, but she didn't have a choice. He was well known in the community, and he knew the job. She had to admit that even the dumbest, meanest bastards in town stood up straight and kept their heads down when Earl walked by. She figured having him around was a nice deterrent, if nothing else.

"Afternoon, Dolores," Earl said, tipping his hat and actually making the old girl blush a little.

"Is he in?" she said, and Dolores nodded.

"But he's made it very clear I'm not supposed to let you in," she said. She lowered her voice a little. "I need this job, Chief."

Dana looked over at Earl, who gave Dolores a wink before doing what he did best, which was roll right over anyone in his way. "I don't give a damn what he's doing," he said in a loud voice. "Either get him out here, or I go in after him."

Sure enough, Mather's door opened at the commotion, and Dolores mouthed a silent "thank you" to them as she looked appropriately distraught. "I'm sorry, Mr. Mather. I tried to tell them you weren't to be disturbed."

"It's okay, Dolores," he said. "You can't expect civilized behavior from uncivilized people. Chief, I'm quite sure I told you I have nothing more to say to you without an attorney present."

"Then Dolores can call and have him meet you at the station," she said. Earl pulled a pair of handcuffs from his belt and stepped forward. "Carl Mather, you're under arrest for obstruction of justice and witness tampering. Hook him up, Earl."

Earl grabbed him by one wrist and turned him around. Mather promptly tried to pull away, and Dana actually cringed. The standard procedure was to issue strong verbal commands and try to gain control of the arms, but Earl was a bit more direct. He simply grabbed Mather by his jacket and slammed him into the wall, hard enough to make the pictures on the opposite wall shake.

"Try that again," Earl said, pulling his arms behind his back. "Please." Mather complied, and Earl cuffed him. If she didn't know better, she'd say Earl almost looked disappointed he didn't fight more as he hauled him out of the office.

"You want to take him out the side?" Earl said. She was about to answer when the last bell rang, and students began to file out into the hallway.

"No," she said. "Take him right out the front door."

"Come on," Mather said. "There's no need to do this in front of the students."

"Oh, I don't know," Earl said. "After all, their folks pay your salary. I'd say they got a right to know what you're up to."

"Just get him in the car," she said. "And Earl, make sure he doesn't have any accidents."

"I'll be gentle with the little lamb," Earl said, shoving him forward as students piled into the hallways. Naturally, they almost immediately began to stack up at the end of the main hallway to watch the show as Earl dragged Mather to the car. She was only mildly surprised when a few started clapping, and by the time she made it out the door, almost all of them were clapping and cheering.

***

"This is ridiculous," Mather said as Earl pulled him out of the car. "Utterly and totally ridiculous. That was completely unnecessary."

"You're breaking my heart," Dana said as she opened the cell door and Earl dragged him inside. "Turn around and face the wall."

Mather did as he was instructed, and Earl unlocked the cuffs. "You get a hair across your ass, and you're gonna have a rough time of it," Earl said as he stepped backwards out of the cage.

"Chief, he just threatened me," Mather said. "You saw that, right?"

115

"Sit down and shut up," she said, shaking her head as Wendall came in from the back. I'll be damned, she thought. He's actually on time for once.

"That who I think it is?" he said, and Earl nodded, grinning like a kid who just got a brand new bike for Christmas.

Dana motioned for them both to join her in her office as Mather sat down on his bunk and sulked. "Close the door," Dana said, and Wendall closed it behind him.

"What's that all about?" he said.

"Obstruction and witness tampering," she said. "Got eight different statements swearing he threatened or coerced people out of reporting crimes on campus."

"No shit," Wendall said. "Let me guess. All the suspects were on the basketball team."

"Starters," Dana said. "They're also among the suicides out in the woods."

Wendall was quiet for a minute, and she could almost see the wheels turning. "Is it just me, or is that a hell of a coincidence?" he said finally, and Earl nodded.

"Been thinking the same thing myself," he said.

"Well, maybe they aren't afraid any more," she said. She shuffled through the statements, looking at dates. "All of these are from the last year," she said. "We're good on statute of limitations."

"You want me to start running these down?" Earl said, and she nodded.

"Get everything you can out of them, but be gentle about it. Try to remember they're just kids, who apparently have been through hell."

"I'm not that rough," Earl said. "Well, not all the time, anyway," he added when they both just stared at him.

"Where do you need me?" Wendall said.

"Patrol," she said. "We still have a town to look after. It's league night at the bowling alley, so I want you out there before they get going good."

"Got it," Wendall said, standing up. He was heading out when the radio squawked.

"Dispatch to Chief Atwater."

"Go ahead, dispatch," she said into the radio.

"Got a disturbance call from the high school," the dispatcher said. "Caller claims a woman has locked herself in the main office and is threatening self-harm."

"Christ on a bike," Earl said.

"Copy that," Dana said, running for the door. "What now?" she said as she jumped behind the wheel. Since the department only had two cars, Earl took his own truck as Wendall jumped in the other.

They made it to the high school in a matter of minutes, and had to practically shove their way through a knot of students until they got to the main hallway.

"Chief," Dolores said. "It's Melody Hagerrman. She came in and shoved me out the door, and locked me out. She's got a can of gasoline, she dumped it all over herself. She says she's going to burn."

"Okay," Dana said. "Is there another way inside that office?"

"Principal Mathers has a door leading out into the quad," she said.

"Do we have a key for that?" Dana asked, and Dolores shook her head.

"It's in my desk," she said.

"Did she have a lighter, matches, anything like that with her?" Wendall asked.

"I didn't see one," she said, "but we confiscate lighters all the time. They're all in my desk drawer."

"Okay," Dana said. "Dolores, why don't you see if you can't get these kids out of here for me?" she said. Dolores nodded and started toward the knot of students. "Wendall, give her a hand, okay?"

"Got it," he said, walking behind her. The group broke up and went outside as Dana approached the door. Behind her, Earl had his .45 out.

"Hang back for a minute," she said. "I'd rather try and talk her down first."

"So would I," he said. "But I'd rather put one in her shoulder than watch her go up in flames." Dana nodded, then rapped on the door.

"Go away," she heard someone sob. "Just go away. It's my fault. It's all my fault."

"Okay," Dana said. "We can talk about it, Melody. Why don't you open the door, and let's talk, okay?"

"No," she said. "I have to do this. It's my fault. I could have stopped them."

"Okay," Dana said. "Well, tell me about that." She waved Dolores over. "Do you have a key?" she whispered, and Dolores shook her head. "Maybe the janitor?"

"He should," she said.

"Go find him for me," she said, and Dolores nodded, running off.

"Go away," Melody sobbed. "You don't understand. I could have stopped them. I knew what they were doing. I could have stopped them, but I didn't."

"Chief, she's winding up," Earl said. "I'm not sure we can wait for that key."

"Take Wendall and go around back," she said. "Wait for my signal, and breach that door. It sounds like she's in the main office, so it should be a straight shot to her from his office door."

"On it," he said. He grabbed Wendall, and went around the building to Mather's private door.

"Melody," Dana said at the door. "Melody, I'd really like to talk to you. Is it okay if I come in?"

"No," she said, still crying. "I have to do this. I have to."

"No, you don't," Dana said. "We've got all kinds of options here, Melody. You don't have to do this."

"I deserve it," she said. "I deserve to be punished. I knew what they were doing, and I didn't say anything."

"We can talk about that, Melody," she said. Dolores came back with the janitor. He handed her a key.

"Okay, get back," she said. "I need both of you to go back outside and make sure none of those kids comes back inside, understand?" They left, and Dana took a deep breath to steady herself.

"Melody?" she said. "Melody, I need to come in and talk to you, you understand?"

"No," Melody said. "You stay out. Just go away and let

me do this.”

“I can't do that, Melody,” she said. “I'm just going to open the door, okay? I just want to talk to you.” She opened the door a crack, and the smell of gasoline immediately hit her. She opened the door and stepped inside slowly.

Melody Hagerrman was standing in the middle of the front office. Her hair and clothes were soaked, and Dana spotted an empty five gallon gasoline can at her feet. She had a Bic lighter in her hand and was holding it out, like a shield.

“Get back,” she said, sobbing as Dana stepped into the office. “Don't come any closer, Chief. I don't want anyone else to get hurt. Just stay back.”

“Okay,” Dana said, holding out her hands. “It's okay, Melody. I just want to talk to you for a minute here, okay? What's going on?”

“I have to do this,” she said. “I have to do this, because I knew and I didn't stop them.”

“What did you know, Melody?” she said. “Who were you supposed to stop?” She heard her radio click twice, telling her Earl and Wendall were in position.

“You don't understand,” she said. “I knew what they were doing. I could have stopped it.”

“Okay,” Dana said quietly. “We can talk about it, but for us to do that, I need to make sure no one's going to get hurt. I don't want to get hurt, and I don't want you to get hurt, either.”

Melody started shaking. She brought her hands together, and Dana's hand went to her radio.

“Go, go, go,” she said. She heard the back door being kicked, and Earl and Wendall came rushing in as Melody was striking the lighter. It sparked, and everything seemed to happen in slow motion; she saw Earl and Wendall coming out of Mather's office as the lighter finally came to life. Melody looked at her for a moment, and Dana had time to wonder why she looked scared instead of determined like most suicides did before she put the flame against her shirt.

“Get back!” Dana said as the fire ignited the gas vapor in

the air, and Earl held Wendall back as the flashover exploded through the office.

CHAPTER SEVENTEEN

"I'm fine," Dana said as the EMT looked her over. "Barely singed me. Check on my officers, please." She sat on a stretcher in front of the school, growing more annoyed by the minute.

"They're fine," he said. "Minor burns. Now, would you settle down and let me take a closer look at you, please?"

"The victim," she said. "Any word on her?"

"They rushed her in," he said. "I'll make you a deal. Let me take a look at you, and I'll check on her for you. Okay? Looks like you might have some flash burns here."

"I'm fine," she said. "Hand's a little singed, that's all."

"Okay, well let me take a quick look at it," he said, and she gave up and let him examine her hand. "Okay, that's actually not too bad. It's gonna blister on you, though. Try to keep it clean when they break open, and you should be fine. You left or right handed?"

"Right," she said, and he nodded.

"Well, there's that," he said. "Like I said, it's going to

blister. Just keep it clean."

"Thanks," she said as Earl walked over to her. His face was shiny, and his mustache was all but gone, but he seemed otherwise unhurt.

"You good?" he said, and she nodded. The burn on her hand was starting to get a little tight, but nothing she couldn't live with. Melody Hagerrman had it worse. "You look like something's bugging you."

"Just something she said," Dana said. "She kept saying she had to do this. That she had to do it, because she knew what they were doing."

"You think she knew those kids were going to kill themselves?" he said. "She didn't seem like the type to ignore something like that."

"No, she didn't," she said. "But that's not what's sticking with me. She didn't say 'I knew what they were going to do.' She said 'I knew what they were doing.' MacNeil said the same thing. Damn near word for word. 'I have to do this. I knew what they were doing.' Hell of a coincidence."

"Ain't like either one was in their right minds at the time," he said with a shrug. "Can't read too much into it."

"I suppose," she said. "How's Wendall?"

"Bitching about his pretty-boy hair," he said with a smile. He looked serious for a moment. "I don't think it's settled in just yet."

"You think you can handle the scene?" she said, and he nodded.

"I may have done it a time or two," he said, and she chuckled. "You're headed out to the hospital, aren't you?"

Dana nodded. "I want to be there if she wakes up," she said.

"If, not when," he said, catching it immediately. She nodded again.

"Hard to imagine someone living through that," she said. "Be honest, might be better off if she didn't." Earl nodded again, looking around the scene. Two kids started to slip under the tape, and he walked off, yelling at them.

"You two best get your narrow behinds back behind that line," he called out, and they actually jumped as they turned back. Shaking her head, she got up and went back inside to check on Wendall.

She found him in the office, photographing the scene, unnaturally quiet as he worked. "How you holding up?" she said from the doorway.

"Not gonna lie, Chief," he said, taking pictures of the burn damage to the floor and the pour patterns of the gasoline. "That was some pretty hairy shit. I worked a few suicides back when I was with the staties. Saw a guy put a shotgun in his mouth and pull the trigger with his toe once. Hell of a strange way for a woman to kill herself."

"Most women overdose, maybe drown themselves," she said. "I've seen a few slit their wrists, but most of those were attention attempts."

"They don't usually make a mess," Wendall said, nodding. "And this is one hell of a mess."

"Just one more thing that doesn't make any damn sense," she said, shaking her head.

"You caught it, too, didn't you?" he said. "She didn't say she knew what they were going to do. Neither did Henry."

"I caught it," she said. "Don't suppose they were just out of it and said it wrong?"

"Been my experience, someone says something right before they kill themselves, it means something," he said. "Even if it's only to them."

"So, if they said what they meant, what do you suppose they were talking about?" she asked. "Who was doing what that they knew about, and how was it bad enough they needed to kill themselves over it?"

"Could they have been talking about the bullying?" he asked, continuing to snap pictures. "Unless those kids were into something bigger."

"Maybe," she said. "No. Hell, I don't know. Maybe I'm just looking for something that isn't there."

"That's not what your gut's saying, though. Is it?" he asked.

"Something's not adding up," she said. "I'm headed to the hospital, see if I can't get anything out of Melody Hagerrman. Earl's got the scene if anything comes up."

"I'm just about finished here," he said.

"Make sure you print the gas can," she said. "At least, what's left of it. I want to know if anyone other than her handled it."

"Will do," he said. "You see what's left of the label? It's clean. I'm betting she bought it new."

"Good catch," she said. "Oh, hey, I almost forgot. Your sister still looking for work?"

"She took a part-time spot at the gas station," he said. "But I think she's still looking for something better."

"Think she could handle the dispatcher's slot?" she asked.

"She's good under pressure," he said. "Ridiculously well organized. If she doesn't have a heart attack when she sees Earl's system, I think she could do it."

"Give her a call, tell her I'd like to talk to her about it," she said. It felt cold to her, but the reality of the situation couldn't be ignored. With Earl back behind a badge and Mark gone, she had an empty slot to fill, and she couldn't forward the phones to county forever. She supposed technically she could put in for the extra slot for a night dispatcher, but honestly the call volume didn't justify it at the moment. Still, she needed a daytime dispatcher, just so that the station wasn't empty while they were out.

She left Wendall to do his job, and went to see what she could get from Melody Hagerrman, assuming she survived that long.

✳✳✳

"Doctor," Dana said as she walked up to the nurse's station. "Chief Atwater. Melody Hagerrman?"

"Yes," he said, motioning for her to come with him.

"So she's alive?" she said, and he nodded.

"I don't know for how much longer," he said. "To be honest, I'm surprised she's made it this long. Full thickness burns over some eighty percent of her body. Even if she survives the trauma, the first good infection will probably kill her. Does she have any family?"

"I don't know," she said. "I can find out."

124

"If she does, you should get them here as soon as possible," he said.

"Can she talk?" she asked, and he shook his head.

"She's in an induced coma," he said. "I don't expect her to make it through the night."

Damn, she thought. "Okay, thank you," she said, shaking his hand. She gave him one of her dwindling supply of business cards. "Will you call me when her condition changes?"

"Sure," he said. "Was this really self-inflicted?"

"Afraid so," she said.

"Damn," he said. "Nasty way to go. Don't see many suicides by fire."

"Seen more than my share lately of any kind," she said, and he nodded.

"I read something about that. Hell of a cluster."

"Don't I know it," Dana said. "Call me when anything changes, please."

"Will do," he said. "Between the two of us, I'd be surprised if you don't hear from me by midnight."

"Thanks," she said, nodding. With nothing left for her to do here, she started back, wondering what the hell was coming next.

"Earl, it's me," she said as she dialed his cell. "Wasn't able to talk to her. Doctor tells me she's probably not going to make it through the night. They've got her in a medically induced coma."

"Probably for the best," he said. "She ain't gonna make it, no point in letting her suffer."

"I know," she said. "Anyone been by to check on our guest?"

"I'm looking at him right now," he said. "Bitching and moaning non-stop since I got in the door."

"What's his problem?" she said.

"Said no one was here to get him coffee," he said with a laugh. "Wendall says his sister will be by to see you in about an hour. You gonna be back by then?"

"Should be," she said, getting in the car. "You know her, right?"

"Who, Bonnie?" he said. "Known her since she was in pigtails. Good kid. Smarter than most of us put together. Nice but doesn't take much crap."

"Sounds good to me," she said. "Think she can handle dispatch?"

"I think she'll slap me upside the head when she sees my setup," he said, and she laughed. "But I doubt you're gonna find anyone much better, especially on short notice."

"Good to know," she said. "I'm getting ready to get back on the road. Let me know if anything comes up."

"Will do," he said as she heard someone talking loudly in the background. "Hold on a second," he said into the phone.

"Shut the hell up or I'm gonna bounce your damn skull off the floor," Earl said, and she cringed. "Sorry, he's pissing and moaning that he wants something to read now, like I'm the damned bookmobile."

"Just try to ignore him," she said. "Heard from his lawyer yet?"

"Actually, yes," he said. "He says that since the charges against him are personal, he can't represent him since he's actually on retainer for the school district. Looks like they're distancing themselves from him."

"Let him talk to the public defender if he wants," she said. "Or call whoever. I don't want anything to bite us in the ass later."

"Got it," he said. "Mind if I smack him around a little? He's getting on my nerves."

"Rather you didn't," she said, laughing as she pulled out of the parking lot and headed for the interstate. "What is it between you two, anyway?"

"Just old business," he said. "See you when you get back."

She ended the call and settled in for the drive back to town, hoping nothing else happened while she was gone.

CHAPTER EIGHTEEN

"PD showed up about ten minutes ago," Earl said. "I put 'em in the back room for some privacy."

"Works for me," she said. "You cuffed him to something, right?"

"He ain't going nowhere," Earl said. "Not unless he's dragging the safe with him. Bonnie's waiting in your office."

"Oh, good," she said. "She been waiting long?"

"About five minutes," he said, shaking his head. "Took a look at the dispatch desk, and I swear to God her eye twitched." He smiled as Dana shook her head.

"Good thing you didn't show her the filing cabinets," she said. "Don't want to scare her off." She patted him on the shoulder and went to her office, already ninety percent sure she was ready to hire the girl waiting for her.

She'd filed an application months ago, but she didn't have anything open at the time. Now she was just hoping she could convince the girl to take the job for what little she could afford to pay her. "Hi," she said as she stepped into the office. "Bonnie, right?"

"Yes, ma'am," she said, standing up. "Bonnie Wendall."

"Right," Dana said. "Well, Bonnie, I've reviewed your application. You seem to be more than qualified. What makes you want to work for the police department?"

"I like a challenge," she said. "And I'd like to put my degree and experience to use for something other than inventory."

"I can understand that," Dana said. "So, let's say you're alone in the station, with someone in the cell, and they start becoming verbally abusive. Is that something that's likely to get under your skin?"

"I have four older brothers," she said with a smile. "Someone would have to get pretty creative to say anything I haven't heard before."

Dana smiled. "Are you comfortable handling a multi-line phone system, a computer, and a radio at the same time?" she said.

"Absolutely," she said. "I actually have some dispatch experience. Not police dispatch; I worked for a messenger service in college. I used a six-line phone system, radio, and computerized tracking system, handling as many as twenty-five different messengers at one time."

"Sounds hectic," she said, and Bonnie smiled.

"Can be until you get used to it," she said. "I was there for a year and a half."

"Shift starts at eight in the morning," she said. "Nine times out of ten, you're out by four, four-thirty at the latest. But there may be times when I need someone here later than that. Is there anything in your personal life that would make that difficult for you? Kids or a husband?"

"Neither one, Ma'am," she said. "You know my brother. Most guys around here are scared to be seen talking to me." Dana smiled; Wendall was the quintessential protective older brother. It was actually charming, but it could also be a problem.

"Do you see that being an issue?" she said. "In this department, the dispatcher is sort of a catch-all position. You're often the only person in the station. Unfortunately, we generally deal with people who are having some of the worst days of their life, and that can make them unpleasant. Now, we're never far away, and I won't allow anyone to harass any employee of this department without ending up in a cell, but it does happen sometimes. Do you think Wendall will behave himself if it does?"

"I can handle him," she said. "And I can take care of myself."

"Four older brothers, right?" Dana said, and she nodded. "Okay. I'm afraid the pay's not great, but it's steady, and it comes with a city benefit package. If you're interested, I'd like to offer you the position."

"Absolutely," Bonnie said.

"I assume you'll need to give notice at your current position?" she said, and Bonnie nodded.

"I would like to, but I'm sure I can work around that," she said. "My shift at the store runs from six to midnight."

"Great," she said. She pulled out one of the employment packets from her desk and opened it up, handing it to her. "Do you have time to fill out some paperwork?"

"I'm free all day," she said.

"Fantastic," she said. "I'll just leave you with this to get started. When you're done, just give it to Earl, and he'll make sure I get it. Welcome aboard," she said, and Bonnie stood up with her to shake hands.

She left the girl to do the admittedly stupid amount of paperwork that came with a city position, and walked out into the main office as Earl led Mather back to the cage.

"You'll see the judge in the morning," his lawyer said. "We'll see to bail then."

"You mean I have to spend the night in this crap hole?" Mather said.

"I'll bring you an extra pillow," Earl said, and Dana shook her head at him slightly.

"Chief, I want to file a formal complaint," Mather said. "Your officer has been verbally abusive to me from the start."

"Duly noted," she said. "In the meantime, dinner will be in about half an hour. You have your choice of a burger from the drive-in, or a cold cut sandwich from the grocery store deli."

"Burger and fries is fine," he said, sitting down on the cot as his lawyer left. "This is ridiculous."

She ignored him and motioned for Earl to join her in the back room. "Bonnie's filling out her paperwork now," she said. "I'll need you to get her up to speed with the system as soon as possible."

"I'll get it straightened up for her," he said.

"And Earl?" she said as he started to leave. "Whatever's going on with you two, it's over, understand? Just leave him be. The absolute last thing I need to deal with right now is a harassment claim, understood?"

"Yes ma'am," he said. "I'll play nice."

"What's going on between you two, anyway?" she asked. "And since it's spilling over into my station, this time I need an answer."

"A woman," he said with a shrug. "Ain't it always? He never got over it."

"Your wife," she said. "Alma."

"Had it bad for her when we were in school," he said. "Never could let it go, even after we were married. When the cancer took her last year, I guess he blamed me."

"Okay," she said. "But it has to end, Earl. If that's gonna be a problem for you, tell me now."

Earl at least thought about it for a minute. "I don't like the sumbitch," he said. "But there won't be any more trouble."

"Good," she said. "Hold the fort, make sure she has anything she needs. I'm going to check in with Wendall."

"He's probably out by the bowling alley," Earl said.

"Thanks," she said as she walked out of the back room. Mather was pouting on his cot. "Call over to the diner and get his dinner ordered," she said. "I'll swing by and pick it up on my way back in."

"Will do," he said.

***

130

She found Wendall in the bowling alley, apparently in the middle of calming down a couple of angry customers.

"I don't care what you're arguing about," he said firmly as they both started trying to explain. "Don't care where it started. Both of you are going to lock up your trucks, leave the keys at the desk, and either call someone to come get you or walk home. Separately," he said, and they both nodded.

She waited until they were on their way before waving to him. "Looked like fun," she said, and he shook his head.

"Knuckleheads," he said with a shrug. "What's up?"

"Wanted to touch base with you," she said. "I just hired Bonnie."

"Good," he said. "She'll get that mess of Earl's in shape in no time."

"I don't doubt it," she said. "Mostly I needed to talk to you a minute. No big secret messing with Tim Wendall's little sister can get you in deep crap."

"She can hold her own," he said.

"Good," she said. "Because I need to know you're not going to go ballistic the first time someone gets a case of the ass with her."

"Like I said, she can hold her own," he said. "Won't be a problem."

"Good," she said. "I've already got Earl pissing people off. I don't need you bouncing people off the sidewalk." Wendall laughed with her, and nodded.

"Mel Hagerrman going to make it?" he asked, and she shook her head.

"Doctor said he was amazed she was still alive at all," he said. "Couldn't talk to her."

"Damn shame," he said.

She was headed out when they heard a commotion outside, and he shook his head. "Damn it," he said. "Should have known those morons couldn't just walk away."

They ran out to the parking lot, where the two men from earlier were shoving each other and yelling.

"Break it up," Dana said in a loud voice, but they were too involved in their argument to listen. She grabbed the closest one by the arm and his shirt collar, pulling him away.

He tried to lunge forward, and she took him down, pinning his arm behind his back as she put a knee on his head. "Stop resisting," she said. "Put your hands behind your back."

"Get the fuck off me, bitch," he snarled, trying to twist away. She locked the cuffs onto the wrist she had, then grabbed the free hand and started pulling it to her, but he continued to resist. Rather than continue trying to outmuscle him, she simply moved around and dropped her knee into his back. He grunted in pain, and she got his arm where she needed it, locking the cuffs in place.

"You can't be that stupid, boy," she heard Wendall say as the other one stood in front of him with his hands up. "Get your butt on the ground before I have to put you there."

She reached for her Taser as he swung, but by the time she had it out, Wendall blocked the big roundhouse shot and clotheslined him, driving him to the ground hard. "Roll over, stupid," Wendall said, shoving him with his boot until he rolled over. He jerked his hands behind his back and cuffed him, hauling him to his feet. Wendall was usually such a big, lovable goof that it was easy to forget that most of his large frame was solid muscle, and he wasn't the least bit afraid to mix it up.

"You good, Chief?" he asked as he practically threw the drunk over the hood of his car one-handed.

"Yeah," she said, hauling the other one to his feet and putting him over the trunk of her car. He kicked at her, catching her in the ankle. "Stop fighting," she said, pulling up on his wrists and slamming his head into the trunk lid by the hair.

"You stay put," Wendall said, slamming his own prisoner down on the hood for good measure. "You make me chase you, and you'll regret it."

The suspect continued kicking and screaming at her, and she stepped to one side as Wendall grabbed him by the arm. "I got him," Wendall said, picking him up and slamming him down on the ground. She took advantage of his stunned state and grabbed his ankles, pulling them up to his back.

"You have a hog tie?" she said, and Wendall nodded.

"You got him?" he said as she put her knee on his

crossed ankles.

"I got him," she said. Wendall went into his car and grabbed the plastic hobbler, slipping the loops around his ankles and clipping it to the chain of his handcuffs. "We'll put him in my car," she said, and he stood up as she opened the door.

"You," he said to the other one, who was starting to stand up. He caught him before he could make a break for it and shoved him into the backseat of his car. "Come on, where were you going to go? You're handcuffed, man."

"Read him," Dana said. "This guy's not going anywhere." Wendall read him his Miranda rights and advised him he was under arrest, then shut the door on him.

They put the hobbled man in her car and she read him his rights, thankful he'd at least shut up. "Is it just me, or is business seriously picking up around here lately?" Wendall said as she shut the door.

"And here I thought small town policing would be boring," she said, thumping the car. "Let's get these two knuckleheads back to the house."

CHAPTER NINETEEN

Dana pulled in behind the station, with Wendall parking two slots down to give them room to handle the suspects. "You want me to walk this guy in first?" he said, and she nodded.

"Leave his cuffs on until we get his buddy inside," she said, and he nodded.

"Gonna get crowded in there," he said, and she nodded.

"I have an idea about that," she said. "Let's get these two secured, and then I'll deal with it." Wendall walked his suspect inside, and Earl came out with him.

"Looks kinda small," Earl said as she opened the back door. "Probably should have thrown him back." Dana laughed in spite of herself.

"Hey," she said. "Listen up. Here's the deal; I can take that off you and let you walk in, or we can carry you inside. It's entirely up to you. You going to behave?"

"Be the smart thing to do," Earl said. "I'm old, and I might drop you a couple times between here and there."

"I'll be good," he said, and Dana nodded. They pulled him out and set him down, and Dana unhooked the hobbler.

"On your feet," Earl said, pulling him up. She could hear Wendall talking to the other one as they brought his friend inside.

"Come on, man," he said. "Look, we're just drunk. Let me go home, I'll sleep it off, and we'll be good."

"I gave you a chance to do just that," Wendall said, shaking his head. "You two boneheads decided you'd rather fight in the parking lot."

"Come on, man," he said, shaking his head.

"Chief, what's the meaning of this?" Mather said as Wendall cuffed the suspect to one side of the cage. Dana opened the door and led the second one in, cuffing him on the other side. "Do I really need to be in here with these two?"

"That's the thing about jail, Mr. Mather," she said. "Sometimes you end up with some unpleasant people. Tell you what," she said. "Come on into my office and talk to me a minute."

"If it gets me away from the smell," he said, waving a hand in front of his face, and she saw both Earl and Wendall looking away so he didn't see them grinning.

She led Mather into her office and told him to have a seat. "Here's the deal," she said. "I'm not supposed to have more than three people in that cage. Right now I'm at capacity, leaving me no room for anyone else if something happens. To be honest, I don't have time to babysit you. I'm going to call your lawyer, and we'll see if we can't get hold of a judge. I'm going to recommend you be granted bail and released for now."

"Thank you," he said. "Finally, a voice of reason in all this."

"Here's the catch," she said. "If I find out you've had any contact whatsoever with any witnesses, I'll throw you back in there and figure it out later. You'll also be facing additional tampering charges."

"I work with most of them," he said. "That will be difficult."

"You honestly expect the school's going to let you come back?" she said, and he shrugged. "I'm also going to call the superintendent and explain the situation. I'd be very much surprised if you're allowed back on school grounds anytime soon."

"Chief, you're going to destroy my career," he said.

"You did that yourself when you decided a sports program was more important than a student being violently assaulted on your campus," she said, trying not to lose her temper. "Officer Wendall, would you escort Mr. Mather back to the cell for now?"

"Sure thing, Chief," Wendall said as he came inside. Mather stood up, and Wendall led him out of the office. The fact she was about to release him made her stomach turn, but she just didn't have the room for him right now, and county wouldn't take anyone charged with non-violent crimes. Reluctantly, she picked up the phone and dialed the public defender's office.

****

"Okay, Mr. Mather," she said, unlocking the door. "Judge decided you weren't a flight risk, so he agreed to release you on your own recognizance. You're free to go for now; your lawyer has all the details for your court date."

"Well, thank heavens," he said, standing up and starting for the door.

"I need to make sure you understand the whole situation," she said, blocking the way out. "The judge imposed some conditions, just like we talked about. If you have any contact with any of the complainants, you'll be rearrested immediately and be facing more charges. You understand? Your lawyer here can explain it further to you."

"I'm not an imbecile," he said in a huff, and she stepped out of the way to let his lawyer lead him out of the station.

"This day just keeps on coming, don't it?" Earl said, and she nodded.

"Bonnie finish up her paperwork?" she asked, and he nodded, retrieving the packet from his desk.

136

"Dotted every 'I' and crossed every 't'," he said. "Even had a chance to give her a quick rundown on the setup."

"And she didn't have a seizure?" she said, looking at the cluttered dispatch desk. "Wendall, you ready to get back out?" she said, and he nodded.

"I can, but I figured someone needs to watch these two clowns."

"I got it," she said. "Earl, you might as well knock off for the day."

"You sure?" he said. "Not like I got anything better going on."

"I can't afford the overtime," she said, shaking her head. "Get some rest. I have a feeling things aren't about to calm down any time soon."

"Holler if these two get a hair across their asses," Earl said, staring them both down. Both men looked down at the floor, and she knew she wouldn't have any trouble out of either one of them.

"I think we'll be fine," she said. Wendall nodded and walked out the back door with Earl, and she turned to the cage.

"Am I gonna have any problems out of you two?" she said, and one of them shook his head. The other one was sitting on the floor, passed out. Reluctantly, she uncuffed him and went inside to help him to the cot. She locked the cage back up and went to her office. She was still waiting for a call from the hospital, expecting to hear that Melody was dead.

She was about to give up and call them when the front door opened. She stepped out into the main office, where a small, elderly woman with the longest braid of pure white hair she'd ever seen stood at the front desk. She was clutching a small black purse, and she looked scared out of her mind.

"Ma'am?" she said. "How can I help you?"

"Are you Chief?" she said in a fairly thick Eastern European accent. "I must speak with the chief."

"I'm Chief Atwater," she said, opening the gate to let her come back. "How can I help you?"

The old woman looked over at the cage, where the drunk who was still awake was watching her with some interest.

"Mind your business," Dana said, and he looked away. "Maybe we could talk in my office," she said, and the old woman nodded. She led her back, giving the drunk a good hard stare to remind him to behave.

"Have a seat, please," she said, motioning to one of the chairs in front of her desk. "How can I help you?"

"My name Ilona Orosz. I need speak to you about my great grandson," she said. She was obviously struggling to keep up with the conversation in English, but she kept going. "He is very sick. In the head sick."

"I see," she said. "Do you believe he might be dangerous to himself or others?"

"Yes," she said. "Very angry. I try to help him, but he very angry. He angry for many years. I think maybe he get better with time, but he still very angry."

"What's he angry about?" she said.

"His," she said, looking frustrated. "I not know word. *Éget hegek*," she said. She looked frustrated for a moment until she saw Dana's left palm. She pointed excitedly. "*Éget hegek*. Like this." She pointed at Dana's hand. "*Éget hegek*."

"I'm sorry, I don't understand," Dana said. "I don't know what language you're speaking. His hand?"

"No," she said. "*Éget hegek*. Like you hand. How you say?"

"Burns?" she said, the wheels finally turning. "He's angry because he's been burned?"

"Yes," the old woman said. "He burned very badly. Over whole of him. Very bad."

"What's his name?" she said, but she already knew exactly who she was talking about.

"Gavin," she said. "My great-grandson. Gavin Anderson. Please help, he very angry. All the time. I am afraid he hurt someone with mind."

"With mind?" she said. "You think he intends to hurt someone?"

"I scared of him," she said quietly. "He like my *nagymama*, my grandmother. He do things with mind. *Boszorkány*," she said, crossing herself. "He witch, like my grandmother, my daughter. But he sick, make him hurt people."

"I see," she said, thinking she really didn't need this much crazy in one day. "So, he's a witch who hurts people with his mind."

"I know sound foolish. I sound like *bolond* old woman to American. But Gavin hurt people. He hurt kids in woods. Kids hurt him, so he hurt back."

"Okay," she said, resisting the urge to shake her head and laugh. "I'll look into it. In the meantime, if you think he's a danger to himself or others, we can check that out, maybe have him put on a psychiatric hold for evaluation."

"Hospital no help," she said, sounding incredibly sad. "Try help before, when burned. He make doctors stop helping, say he not sick. He make people do what he want. Kids in woods, kids at graves. Man and woman from school. He make them hurt themselves."

"You're telling me he made them kill themselves?" she said, and this time she couldn't keep the doubt out of her voice. "How exactly did he manage that?"

"Is hard to say," she said, shaking her head. "I no understand how explain *boszorkány*. Most not bad. He not bad, he sick. He good boy before burn. But he dangerous now. Need stop."

Deciding she wasn't getting rid of her without playing along, Dana nodded. "I'll tell you what I can do," she said. "I can go talk to him. If he seems like he might be a danger to himself or others, I can have him put on a psych hold, but that's all I can do. Because as far as I can prove, he's not committed any crime."

"He *boszorkány*," she said. "He trick you, like others. You stop him." She started crying, and she reached into her purse for a tissue. "I love him. He good boy, but he sick. He no get better. You must stop."

"I'll go talk to him," she said, thinking she'd eat her desk lamp if it meant this conversation could end. The old woman stood up, looking sad as Dana saw her out.

"I hope you see," she said. "I hope you see before too late. He good boy, but you must stop before he hurt more.

He so angry."

"I'll do what I can," Dana said. "Thank you for coming in. Do you have a way home?"

"My granddaughter drive me," she said, pointing to a car across the street.

"Gavin's mother?" she said, and the old woman nodded as she got out of the car and came over to help her.

"Afternoon," Dana said. "Mrs. Anderson?"

"Sonya," she said. "Grandma, why don't you go wait in the car, and I'll be there in a minute?"

"He good boy, Chief. But he sick. He hurt. You must stop," she said.

"Okay, Grandma," she said. "I'll talk to her." The old woman looked at them both for a moment, then walked carefully across the street and got in the car.

"I'm sorry," Mrs. Anderson said. "She gets confused sometimes. I imagine she told you a heck of a story."

"She seems to think Gavin might be a danger, to himself or others," she said. "Is that a fair assessment?"

"He's angry," she said, shrugging. "He's had problems since his father died; who wouldn't? But he's not crazy."

"Okay," Dana said. "Does she live with you?"

"Yeah," she said. "For now, anyway. She gets confused a lot, and it's getting harder to take care of her."

"There are resources that can help," she said, and Mrs. Anderson nodded.

"I'm talking to them," she said. "I'm sorry she bothered you."

"No bother at all," Dana said. "She seems like a nice lady."

"She is," she said. "Just gets confused easily. I'd better get her home."

"You have a good evening," Dana said, making sure she was inside before shaking her head.

"Crazy old broad," the drunk in the cage said.

"Shut up," she said, going back to her office.

CHAPTER TWENTY

She stuck around until Wendall came in to do his shift report. "How you guys feeling?" she said, standing in front of the cage as the two drunks inside woke up.

"Guessing I've been better," the one who'd passed out first said as he sat up. "Petey, what the hell'd we get into this time?"

"Guessin' by the shiner you got and my fat lip, I'm thinkin' we started beatin' on each other," Petey said.

"I'm gonna go out on a limb here and guess neither one of you's very interested in pressing charges," she said.

"Nah," Petey said.

"Mom'd kick our butts," the other one said.

"Wait," Dana said. "You guys are brothers?"

"You didn't know?" Wendall said, and she just shook her head. "Guess you guys have been behaving for a few years, huh?"

"Yeah," Petey said. "Usually do our drinking at home these days."

"Probably a good call," Dana said. "Look guys, simple truth is I don't have anyone to sit with you tonight, and I can't leave you here alone. That means I have two choices. I can either see if county's got room for you, or I can issue you both citations for drunk and disorderly and send you home. Honestly, I'm tired and I don't feel like driving you up to county tonight."

"We'll pay the tickets," Petey said, and his brother nodded.

"I need to make myself clear here, fellas," she said. "We both witnessed the assaults, so technically I don't need either of you to press charges. I'm cutting you guys a break because honestly I have other things to deal with. Don't make me regret it, okay?"

"No ma'am," Petey said.

"Won't be a problem," his brother said, and Dana nodded.

"You boys got someone who can come get you?" she said, and they nodded.

"Your uncle Carl?" Wendall said, and Petey nodded. "I'll give him a call."

"Thanks, Wendall," she said. "If I leave you boys to get home, are you going to give Deputy Wendall any trouble?"

"No ma'am," Petey said. "I think he's probably about tired of smacking us around by now."

"Ain't that the truth," Wendall said, and she nodded. She walked over to his desk, out of earshot.

"You know these guys," she said. "You have a problem cutting them loose on a D and D?"

"Nah," he said. "They're actually pretty good guys when they're sober. They'll straighten up." He smiled and spoke up. "Hell, they'll be on their best behavior when their uncle gets here, just so he doesn't thump them both."

"He's not wrong, Chief," Petey said.

"Okay," she said. "Go ahead and call him for them. If they behave until he gets here, cut 'em loose."

"I got it from here, Chief," he said. "Travis will be on soon."

"Good night," she said. She started for the door, but

stopped when her phone rang. She resisted the urge to groan as she went back to the office and answered it.

"Chief, this is Dr. Harvey at county general," the caller said. "I'm calling about a patient by the name of Melody Hagerrman."

"Yes," she said. "Has her condition changed?"

"I'm afraid Ms. Hagerrman coded thirty minutes ago," he said. "Attempts to resuscitate her were unsuccessful."

"Okay," she said, nodding. "Thank you for calling." She hung up and dragged herself out into the main office as the day finally caught up to her.

"Melody Hagerrman?" Wendall said when he saw her face, and she nodded. "Damn."

"I'm going to go get some sleep," she said.

"Won't be far behind you," he said. "Good night, Chief."

She stopped just long enough to give a final admonishment to Petey and his brother, then drove home on autopilot. The house was empty when she got there, and she wasn't sure if that was a good or a bad thing. She decided it didn't have to be either, and managed to stay awake just long enough to put away her gear before crawling up the stairs and collapsing into bed.

***

"Hey, Chief?" Earl said as she started for her office. "Got something you might want to see."

"Give me a second to grab some coffee," she said around a yawn. "Jesus, how are you always so awake?"

"Really don't think this can wait, Dana," he said, and she stopped with her hand on the doorknob. He'd never addressed her by first name, not once in all the years she'd known him. She froze in place when she heard an unmistakable sound; the hammer of a 1911 being cocked back.

"Earl, what's going on?" she said, turning around slowly. Earl had his pistol in his hand, down at his side. "Earl, I don't think there's anything going on that requires you to draw your sidearm." He just shrugged at her, looking

143

confused.

"Earl, holster your weapon," she said firmly.

"They had it coming, Chief," Earl said. "Every one of the rotten cocksuckers had it coming. They all have it coming. Even me," he said, grinning.

She saw it all happen in slow motion. Earl grinned at her again as he put the pistol under his chin.

"Wait," she said, trying to get to him. It felt like she was being held back, struggling to get to him as he thumbed the safety off.

"Everything works out in the end, Dana," he said. "Everyone gets what they got coming."

She screamed as Earl pulled the trigger, and she woke up as the top of Earl's head splattered against the slowly turning ceiling fan.

****

"Shit," she said as she rolled over and looked at the alarm clock. It was barely four in the morning, and she was wide awake. She sat up and ran a hand through her hair, waiting for the shakes to stop as the nightmare faded. Eventually she got up and peeled off her sweat-drenched uniform, dragging herself to the shower.

Dressed in sweats and a tank top, she started for the bedroom, but ended up in the kitchen instead. She started a pot of coffee and looked to see if there was anything that could reasonably be called breakfast in the house.

She was just about to settle for the brownies Macy had no doubt brought over at some point when the security lights in the backyard fired up. Shit, she thought as she realized her sidearm was locked up in the hallway closet safe.

Thankful for her more paranoid moments, she reached into the gap between the fridge and the wall, finding the little Mossberg .410 pump shotgun in the rack she'd bolted to the wall for it. She chambered a shell and checked to make sure the batteries on the flashlight clamped to the tube magazine were still working, and headed for the back door, killing the kitchen light. She didn't want to be backlit in the doorway.

144

She scanned the backyard as far as the lights reached, which was only about half-way out. Any farther, and they'd disturb the neighbors.

"Come out with your hands up and empty," she said, the shotgun held at low ready. Reluctantly, she turned on the weapon light and stepped off the porch, checking the dark corners of the yard.

She jumped at a noise behind her, and came within inches of blasting the neighbor's cat with a load of buckshot. She let out a shaky breath as the cat looked at her for a minute before sauntering off on whatever business it was out for.

At least everyone's still asleep and didn't see me out here making an ass of myself, she thought as she let the shotgun dangle at her side. Feeling like an idiot, she went back inside, locking the back door before removing the shell from the shotgun's chamber and slipping it back into the loading gate. She put the shotgun back in the wall mount and poured a cup of coffee before curling up on the couch.

She supposed it wasn't a surprise she was having bad dreams; between the horrors she'd seen over the last few days, the long hours, and the admittedly spooky story from the old woman, she was bound to be a little on edge.

On impulse, she picked up her tablet off the coffee table. "What the hell was that word?" she asked out loud. Eventually she just typed in "eastern European witches" and started reading. After the fifth article talking about witches and monsters, she gave up and set the tablet down.

"Just a crazy old woman," she said, shaking her head. She'd see about talking to Gavin Anderson today, though; crazy old superstitions or not, the woman had said she believed he was unbalanced and a danger. She was obligated to talk to him and see for herself.

She thought it best to leave out the part about him being a witch, unless she wanted to end up playing checkers with him in the day room of the psych unit.

Eventually she decided she'd lounged around the house

145

long enough, and went upstairs to get dressed. She was fidgeting with her duty belt when someone knocked on the door. There was really only one person who'd be stopping by at six in the morning, but Macy wouldn't just come in without knocking first. It was partly to respect her need for privacy, but also because someone walking in without knocking would have her reaching for her firearm.

She opened the door, smiling. "Morning," she said as Macy stepped inside, waiting for the door to close before giving her a kiss and holding up a bag of donuts.

"Long night?" she said, getting a good look at her.

"Shows that badly?" Dana asked, and Macy shook her head.

"Nah," she said. "I just know you. That, and I saw your car in the station parking lot last night when I went for a run."

"Still running in the middle of the night?" she said, and Macy grinned.

"Ten o'clock is hardly the middle of the night," she said. "And I'm a big girl. I can take care of myself, Chief."

"Point taken," she said as she slipped her arms around Macy's waist. "You could have stopped in and said hi."

"And get a lecture on running alone at night?" she said with a grin, and Dana shrugged.

"I'm a worrier," she said. "It's what I do."

"Besides, anything that has you there that late at night is usually bad news," she said. "Figured I'd just be in the way."

"Never," Dana said.

"Anyway, I just wanted to stop by and see how you're holding up," she said, looking at her bandaged left hand. "I heard you were right there when it happened."

"I'm okay," she said. "I know how that sounds, but I'm okay, really."

"Well, school's shut down," Macy said. "At least for the kids. We're supposed to show up for some sort of staff meeting. Probably to talk about what we're supposed to say to the kids when they ask."

"Did you know her very well?" Dana asked, and Macy nodded.

"Yeah," she said. "She was one of the good ones. Knew the score, but was still green enough to actually care about her job."

"I know the type," she said, thinking of Wendall. "Mind if I be a cop for a second and ask you something?"

"Depends," she said, biting her lip. "If I say no, you promise to wrestle me to the ground?" Dana smiled with her. "Shoot."

"You think Melody knew the full extent of what Chase and the others were doing?" she said. "The bullying, the arsons, all of it?"

"I hate to think she did and didn't say anything," Macy said, "but I suppose it's possible. She needed the job as much as anyone else."

"Was Gavin Anderson their only target?" she asked, and Macy shook her head as she leaned up against the back of the couch.

"Not by a long shot," she said. "He was definitely one of their favorites, but they spread it around. Hell, you know kids, especially if they think they're untouchable."

"Honest impression," Dana said. "Gavin strike you as dangerous at all? Maybe unstable?"

"Hard to say," she said with a shrug. "And that's not just me being coy. He was always angry as a kid, but who isn't, right? Mind if I ask you a question?"

"Depends," she said, smiling. "You gonna wrestle me to the ground?"

"I had that one coming," Macy said, laughing. "But seriously. What is it that makes you keep coming back to Gavin? I mean, sure. He's connected to the suicide victims, granted. But so is half the town."

"Honestly, I wish I knew," Dana said. "Just a nagging hunch that won't go away."

"Well, if I know your hunches half as well as I think I do, then there's probably something there. Now, sit down and eat before you go in. It's bad form to arrest someone with your stomach growling."

CHAPTER TWENTY-ONE

"How'd your night go?" Earl said with a knowing smile.

"Okay, what did you hear?" she said, shaking her head as she poured a cup of coffee.

"Heard you finally met old Ilona," he said, laughing. "Always good for a laugh, that one."

Dana nodded, smiling. "She always been such a character?"

"Got worse over the last few years," he said. "Nice old gal. She could tell you some stories, too. What'd she tell you?"

"She thinks Gavin might be mentally ill," she said, and he nodded.

"She ain't the only one to think it," he said. "Hell that kid's been through, it'd be a damned miracle if he wasn't a little out to lunch."

"You want to know what caught my attention?" she said, ignoring the craziest parts of the old woman's story. "She thinks he might have had something to do with these suicides."

"Kinda contrary, ain't it?" he said. "How you suppose he managed all that?"

Screw it, she thought. He'd get a kick out of it, and it wasn't like she'd actually believed her. "You ready for this? She thinks he's some kind of witch. Says he made them do it with his mind."

"What, like talked them into it?" he said, and she shook her head.

"I don't think that's where she was headed with it," she said. "Sounded more like he thinks it, they do it. Said I had to stop him. Crazy as all hell."

"Usually," he said. "I take it we're attending the memorial service this morning?"

The families would all have their own private funeral services, and there were a couple she intended to attend, but the town itself was holding a memorial service in the park later this morning.

"I think it might be a good move," she said. Mark's funeral would be later in the week, and she didn't think she'd be able to keep the guys away from it for anything, so she had no intention of trying.

Earl studied her for a minute. "You're still not satisfied about something," he said. "You don't think there's something else going on here, do you? Walt himself said there's nothing saying any of those folks met with any bad intentions."

"I know," she said, shaking her head. "Just can't get past the feeling we're missing something."

"I think maybe you're just a little allergic to easy explanations," he said, and she shrugged.

"Probably," she said. "Still, she said the magic words. She made it clear she thinks he might be a danger to himself, or others. Gonna have to talk to him."

"A body could make the same case for old Ilona," he said quietly. "Nice enough old gal, but it ain't exactly a secret she ain't all there these days."

"Maybe," she said. "You didn't see her last night, though. I think she's genuinely scared."

"Well, he's liable to show up at this little shindig," he said. "Nothing says we can't pull him aside and have a chat."

"Suppose we should," she said as Bonnie came through the door, right on time.

"Good morning, Chief," she said. "Detective."

"Shoot," he said with a grin. "We're gonna get along, you're gonna have to stop treating me with any sort of respect." Dana smiled but didn't laugh, not wanting to encourage the old guy. "Call me Earl."

"Okay then," Bonnie said. "Where should I start?"

"I'll be on the radio," Dana said. With Mark gone and Earl getting Bonnie squared away on the systems, patrol was left up to her. She didn't mind; it beat sitting at her desk and fighting the endless mountain of paperwork.

"Service starts at eleven," he said. "That'll give me just about enough time to get Miss Bonnie here up to speed. Meet you at the park?"

Dana nodded. "Oh, Bonnie," she said. "I should probably ask. Are you at all adverse to handling firearms?"

"Well, I don't have a lot of experience, but I'm not against it or anything," she said. "Is it required for the job?"

"Not at all," Dana said. "But there will be times you're alone here, and I'm not going to tell you not to do anything you feel necessary to stay safe. If you're interested, we can get you up to speed. If you'd rather, we can certify you with the TASER or pepper spray."

"Let me think about the gun," she said after a moment, and Dana nodded her appreciation. It wasn't a decision to be made lightly. "But I think at least the TASER would be a good idea."

"I'll get you signed up for the class," she said. "Meanwhile, there should be one in the desk. Earl can at least give you the basics of it for now."

"You're gonna love it," Earl said, smiling. "Ever seen a three hundred pound man dance like a chicken?"

"Behave, you two," she said, smiling as she went out on morning patrol.

***

"Tell you what," Dana said, looking down at the moderately terrified kid sitting behind the wheel of entirely too much car for him. "You give me your word you'll keep it at the speed limit, and we'll let it go with a warning this time," she said. "Sound good to you?"

"Yes ma'am," he said quickly, looking like he wanted to pass out. "I'll be good."

"Good to hear," she said. "It's a nice car. Hate to see you wrap it around a pole. Be careful, okay?" she said, handing him the written warning form.

"Yes ma'am," he said, and she thumped the top of the car gently as she walked back to her patrol car. He'd only been going ten miles over the limit, but her main point in stopping him hadn't been generating the ticket, but maybe scaring him into driving safely for a bit longer. Judging by the look of relief on his face, she figured she'd bought at least two hours of safe driving for her trouble.

She watched until the nervous kid drove off, signaling the closest turn, and pulled back out into traffic. With school out for the next day or so at least, the kids were out in full force, hanging out in the park or at the drive-in. She took a turn through the park, more to be seen than actually looking for trouble, and then swung by the drive-in.

Other than a very small scuffle which broke up as soon as she pulled into the parking lot, there was nothing going on. She stayed long enough to order a soda just in case the gladiators weren't done just yet, and by the time she paid and tipped the waitress, it was time to make her way back to the park. The memorial service would be starting in about thirty minutes, and she wanted to be there early enough to get a good look at everyone as they arrived.

She saw Earl take up a position near the entrance, so she hung back at the rear. Between the two of them, they'd be visible enough to deter any foolishness, while still in position to see anything out of the ordinary. She wasn't sure exactly what she was looking for, but her gut was screaming at her that something was wrong. Maybe she was just spooked by the old woman's story. Hell, maybe Earl was right, and she was just allergic to easy answers.

Speaking of which, she spotted Mrs. Anderson leading her mother to the chairs the parks department had set up for the event. Ilona looked dignified and stoic, but underneath it wasn't hard to see she was terrified. It also wasn't hard to see why; Gavin, dressed in a white dress shirt and black slacks, sat on the other side of her, between her and the crowd like any other protective young man would have done.

She couldn't help but notice the way people cut a wide swath away from them, some of them not even bothering not to stare. She felt bad for him, but he seemed to take it in stride. He leaned down to listen to something Ilona said, and he nodded, patting her arm before standing up and walking back to the parking lot.

She pulled out her cell and dialed Earl's number. "Earl, Gavin's coming your way," she said. "I want to know what he's up to."

"I got him," Earl said. "Looks like he went back to the car to fetch his shawl." She chuckled and shook her head. "Headed back to you."

"I see him," she said as Gavin came back. He spread the shawl over Ilona's shoulders before sitting back down. Someone said something to the old woman from the next row up, and she nodded.

"Chief, I gotta say this. If he's a wrong guy, he's sure playing the role pretty good," he said. "Ain't many deranged killers that fetch shawls for little old ladies."

"I know," she said. "If this thing goes off without a hitch, I'll make contact and see if he seems like a danger to anyone."

"And if he don't?" he said.

"Then I guess I'm just imagining things, and we'll move on," she said.

"Got someone else headed your way," he said. "Imagine she'll get your attention off the boy."

"Just keep your eyes open for trouble," she said, laughing as she ended the call. Macy walked up to her, looking respectable but still all manner of hot in a black dress and heels Dana would have killed herself trying to walk in.

"Hi," she said, putting the phone away. "You look great."

"Thanks," Macy said. She wanted to take her hand for a minute, but she was in uniform. The whole issue of her orientation aside, she should at least try to keep up a professional appearance. She could tell by the look on Macy's face she understood, and she was thankful for it. "I take it you're working, and not just attending the service?"

"A little of both," Dana said, keeping Gavin in her view. Macy followed her look, and nodded.

"You still think he had something to do with all this?" she said quietly.

"Tell you the truth, I'm beginning to think I'm just chasing wild geese," she said.

"Well, good luck," Macy said as a group of teachers waved to her. "I should get back. You going to be off tonight?"

"Barring any more tragedies," she said. "God, I didn't just jinx the whole thing, did I?"

"Let's hope not," Macy said. She brushed her hand lightly for just a moment, and went back to join the others. Dana took a deep breath and made sure Gavin was still in his seat before scanning the rest of the crowd.

"Let's hope not," she repeated, hoping like hell things went back to normal soon. Her pulse quickened a bit as Gavin stood up, but she relaxed when she realized he'd simply given up his seat to another old lady, who chattered quietly with Ilona as he stepped to the rear with the rest of the mourners who'd elected to stand.

"What are you up to?" she said quietly, watching him as he watched the crowd. It wasn't the normal people-watching of someone bored at a public function. He seemed to be looking for someone. Whoever it was, he must have spotted them, because he started making his way around the outside of the crowd.

She followed him, keeping back far enough to not be seen. She was more than a little surprised to see who he was talking to; Gavin stood off to the side of the crowd with Mayor Shelby, speaking in hushed tones. She watched as they had what to all appearances was a normal, casual chat until one of the local ministers stepped up onto the bandstand and tapped awkwardly on the mic.

Mayor Shelby made his excuses, shook Gavin's hand, and started for the bandstand to take his place as Gavin moved forward enough to see.

He didn't wear a hat, and the rough pink scar tissue that covered half his bald head made him easy to spot as he moved. She stayed with him, pulling out her phone. "Earl, you got eyes on the bandstand?" she said.

"Right behind it, coming around the side," he said. "We got trouble?"

"I don't know," she said. "Keep an eye on the Mayor. I just saw him talking to Gavin."

"Yes ma'am," he said, ending the call. He was polite enough, but it wasn't hard to tell he thought she was probably losing her marbles. Hell, for all she knew she really was losing it. So far there was absolutely nothing about the young man that gave her any sort of justification for suspecting him of anything but being a decent guy who'd been dealt a truly crappy hand in life.

"Morning, Chief," someone said behind her. She turned to see Wendall in an actual suit and tie, standing next to his wife as she held their daughter.

"Morning," she said, smiling at the little girl. "Don't you look pretty," she said, and the girl blushed.

"Sophie, what do you say?" Wendall said.

"Thank you," the little girl said, grinning.

"You remember my wife, Annie," he said, and Dana nodded, smiling.

"Not likely to forget anyone who can make this big lug behave," she said, and Annie laughed. Dana stepped aside enough to keep Gavin in her line of sight without turning her back on them, and it didn't escape Wendall's attention.

"Helps if you control the meatloaf supply," Annie said, and Dana laughed quietly with her. She saw where they were both looking, and nodded. She didn't seem annoyed, which meant she knew why Wendall had come in the first place.

"We'll just go find a seat," Annie said, and Wendall

nodded, giving her a polite kiss before taking Sophie from her and giving the girl a big hug.

"You be good for Mommy, okay Bug?" he said, and Sophie nodded. "Give me one, right here," he said, touching his cheek. Sophie gave him a big kiss, and he handed her back to Annie. After they'd left, he turned back to Dana.

"Figured you were still all twisted up over something," he said. "Thought you could use another pair of eyes."

"Make that two," Travis said as he walked up to them.

"You guys don't have to be part of this," she said. "You're off duty."

"No such thing," Travis said, and she finally noticed that both were carrying their sidearms under their jackets. "You want one of us to get close to him?"

"Quietly and carefully," she said. "If anything happens, hold onto him."

"On what charge?" Wendall said as the minister began praying. "Don't get me wrong, I got the same bad feeling you do. Just can't go grabbing citizens on bad feelings, though."

"Material witness," she said. "Just like everyone else." Wendall nodded, and Travis clapped him on the shoulder.

"I'll take it," he said. "You're liable to step on someone underfoot, you big gorilla." Dana smiled as Travis made his way up to where Gavin stood, his head bowed with the rest of the crowd.

"His mother and great-grandmother are on the other side, near the aisle," she said. "Stick close to her, make sure she gets out okay if there's panic."

"You're really expecting trouble, aren't you?" he said, and she nodded.

"Wish I wasn't, but yeah," she said. "Something's not right here."

She had no idea what it might be, but she couldn't ignore her gut any more. There was something very weird going on, and she'd bet her pension Gavin Anderson was at the middle of it all.

CHAPTER TWENTY-TWO

With Travis on Gavin and Wendall watching the old woman, she made her way toward the front of the crowd, where she found Earl standing just off to the side of the bandstand, watching the crowd.

"The boys find you?" he said, and she nodded.

"You do that?" she said, and he shook his head.

"Not me," he said. "They came on their own. I guess you're not the only one with a bad feeling."

"What about you?" she said. "You have a bad feeling, too?"

"I've always got a bad feeling," he said. "That way I'm not surprised when I'm right. Take that, for instance," he said, nodding toward the bandstand. "You ever known Shelby to be able to stand still for this long?"

"Not really," she said. Mayor Shelby was known for constantly being on the move, even at events where he was expected to speak. He usually preferred to mingle with the crowd until time for him to speak, but today he stood quietly behind the minister as he read down the list of victims.

She saw Travis standing a few feet away from Gavin, who was watching the minister. He was paying rapt attention, nodding slightly at each name. Over on the other side of the crowd, she could see Ilona watching him as well. She looked over at Dana, and there was no misunderstanding the look on her face; the old woman was terrified. She had a death grip on her granddaughter's arm, and her lower lip was quivering slightly.

"She's scared," Dana said. Earl looked over at Ilona, and nodded.

"Scared of something, that's for sure," he said. "Question is, what? Or maybe who?"

"Three guesses," she said, watching as Gavin nodded when the minister read off Chase Garner's name. The minister finished up with another short prayer, and a heart-felt plea to listen to the children.

"Please," he said. "When your children try to tell you something is wrong, listen to them. They're asking us for help. We can't afford to fail them again."

A smattering of applause greeted him, and he stepped away from the podium. "Here we go," Earl said. "Bet he goes on for at least half an hour."

"Maybe longer," she admitted. She watched as Mayor Shelby stepped up to the podium, adjusting the mic and straightening his tie as he cleared his throat.

"Thank you, Reverend," he said. "That was lovely." Another small round of applause came, and he took a moment before continuing, presumably getting his thoughts together. Travis gave her a small nod to let her know he was still on Gavin. Wendall did the same, keeping an eye on Ilona, and she made herself relax just a little. She was wound up too tightly, as if she were waiting for all hell to break loose.

"I had a nice little speech all prepared for today," Mayor Shelby said, "but standing here in front of you fine people this morning on such a somber occasion, it just doesn't seem right. Instead, I think I'll just share with you my thoughts.

"Whenever a single young life is lost, the tragedy is almost unbearable.   When so many are lost, that tragedy is magnified. We find ourselves asking 'why? How could such a thing happen?' We blame ourselves, and sometimes each other." He looked out at the crowd for a minute, and several of them looked uncomfortable.

"We ask ourselves how we could have possibly missed the signs. Honestly, I'd like to stand up here and tell you there was nothing any of us could have done to prevent this terrible thing from happening, but I'd be lying. I'd be lying, because some of us knew what was happening. We knew what they were doing, and we did nothing to stop it."

"Shit," Dana said under her breath as she recognized the wording. "Earl, something's wrong." Good old Earl, who might occasionally tell her when she was being a fool, just nodded and started for the front of the bandstand as Mayor Shelby produced a snub-nosed revolver from his pocket.

A woman screamed as he cocked the hammer back and pressed the barrel against his temple. "I knew what they were doing. I could have stopped them."

"Mayor," Dana said, drawing her weapon at the same time Earl did. "Stop. Let's talk about this. Put the gun down."

"I have to do this," he said. "Don't try to stop me. You'll never be able to stop me."

"I got no shot," Earl said. "Everyone get the hell out of there," he said. The few people on the bandstand started going over the railing, and Shelby stepped forward.

"I have to do this," he said again. "I don't have a choice. Please, just get out of the way."

"Chief," Earl said, waiting for her to give him the go-ahead.

"Patrick," Dana said. "Listen to me. Listen to my voice, okay? You don't have to do this. Just put the gun down." Fuck it, she thought. Worth a shot. "Don't let him do this to you," she said quietly. "Help me stop him."

"I knew what they were doing," he said. "Everyone knew what they were doing. Everyone knew, and no one tried to stop them. Everyone knew, everyone pays."

"Hands," Earl shouted as Shelby reached into his pocket.

He held up something; it took her a moment to understand it was almost certainly a detonator. "Chief? Gonna have to make a call here."

"Take him," she said. Earl fired twice in rapid-fire succession. Two large .45 caliber slugs hit Shelby, one in each shoulder. The gun and detonator both fell away from him as Shelby hit the floor of the bandstand.

"Clear," Earl said, kicking the gun away as Dana picked up the detonator.

"Wireless," she said. "Get everyone out of here," she said as people were starting to come out of their shocked silence.

"Okay, everyone back," Earl said in his booming voice. The crowd stepped back several feet almost on reflex, and it didn't take him long to move everyone back about a hundred yards to the other side of the park. She looked over and saw Travis had Gavin by one arm. Wendall was leading Ilona over to him.

"I have to do this," Shelby said, groaning in pain as he tried to sit up. She put him back down on the floor of the bandstand, cuffing his hands in front of him before hauling him to his feet.

"Where's the bomb, Patrick?" she said. "Tell me where the bomb is."

"I have to do this," he said, shaking his head. "I don't have a choice. I have to do this. Let me go, I have to do this."

"Where is it?" she asked again. Reluctantly, she pulled on one arm, making him squeal at the pain. It worked; he at least stopped babbling.

"Help me," he said, sobbing. "I don't want to do it, but I have to."

"Don't let him do this," Dana said quietly. "It's Gavin, isn't it? He's the one making you do this, isn't he?"

"Help me," he said again.

"Tell me where the bomb is," she said.

"Under," he said, gasping in pain. "Under the bandstand. I'm sorry," he said.

"Help me stop him," she said.

"No, you don't understand," he said. She should have been paying more attention, but she was distracted chasing a theory. When Shelby clasped his hands together and swung them at her jaw, it caught her off guard and knocked her down.

"Chief!" Earl shouted as Shelby picked up the detonator she'd dropped.

"Run," Shelby said as he climbed back up the stairs to the bandstand. "He doesn't want you. You didn't know. Run, now," he said. He'd knocked her down and gotten far enough away that she'd never get to him in time. With nothing left to do, she got to her feet and sprinted toward the horrified crowd. She heard someone scream again, and she had just enough time to realize Shelby must have pressed the button before something slammed into her from behind, sending her rolling across the lawn.

She rolled over, stunned as fire shot into the sky, carrying most of the bandstand with it. She watched as Mayor Shelby disappeared in a ball of fire, and she was vaguely aware she couldn't hear anyone screaming as someone grabbed her under the arms and pulled her away.

Pieces of the bandstand rained down on the park; a section of banister buried itself in the ground in front of her a foot deep, charred and smoking. Something wet splatted down next to her, and it took her mind a moment to recognize the shape. It was a foot, the shoe missing as the black socks smoldered.

She gave up fighting it and passed out as whoever had her continued to drag her away from the falling debris.

***

"Jesus fucking wept," someone said as Dana opened her eyes. Someone had her head in their lap, and it took her a moment for her eyes to focus enough to see Macy looking scared out of her mind as she stared down at her. "You. Get the hell back behind that tape or you're going to jail," someone said, and she recognized Earl's voice.

"She's awake," Macy said, crying as she held onto her

160

hand. Two impossibly large figures blocked out the sun as they stood over her.

"Chief?" Wendall said. "Just sit tight, okay? Bus is on the way."

"I'm fine," she said, trying to sit up and almost passing out.

"You just stay put," Travis said, gently but firmly holding her down. It would have normally pissed her off, but she was too tired and disoriented to argue with anyone at the moment. She could hear ambulance sirens in the distance, and was a little impressed they'd gotten here so quickly.

"Where is he?" she said, closing her eyes for a moment.

"Mayor Shelby?" Wendall said. "He's gone. Blew himself all to hell." She shook her head, wincing at the pain. More surprising than the pain in her head was the pain in her back; the skin felt hot, and seemed to be too tight, like a bad sunburn.

"Gavin," she said. "Where's Gavin Anderson?"

"He gave me the slip in the confusion," Travis said. "I'm sorry, Chief. I lost him."

"We need to find him," she said.

"You need to stay down and wait for the ambulance," Macy said. "You're officially off duty."

"Was anyone else hurt?" she said, finally forcing her eyes open.

"Couple of minor burns," Wendall said. "A few people hurt by debris, nothing serious."

"Make sure they're treated first," she said.

"That's up to the EMTs," Macy said. "You're hurt worse than they are."

"Help me up," Dana said, finally managing to sit up. She winced at the pain, and Macy shook her head.

"Damn it, Dana," she said, crying. "Stop it. Just stop. Stop being so fucking tough for five minutes and let them take care of you. Please," she added, and that did it. Dana gave up and sat still as the EMTs came running up to them. She let them load her into the ambulance, letting herself relax as Macy climbed in next to her. She reached out and took her hand.

"We're gonna make people talk," Macy said, and Dana just shrugged.

"Screw 'em," she said. "I just got blown up. I get to hold my girlfriend's hand."

"Oh, so that's all it takes," Macy said, and Dana laughed as the EMT climbed into the ambulance. "If I'd only known."

"Ow, don't make me laugh," she said. "My back hurts like a son of a bitch."

The EMT rolled her over carefully. "Looks like second and maybe third degree burns," he said. "You'll have some scarring."

"Never was one for swimsuits anyway," she said. Macy squeezed her hand once more, and she finally let herself pass out again.

CHAPTER TWENTY-THREE

She woke up and realized she was either stoned out of her gourd, or already dead. The pain was gone, and she felt like she was floating as she opened her eyes. "Well, I gotta say, I was hoping to see someone a little prettier," she said as she saw Earl sitting by the bed.

"She went to get something to eat," he said. "She'll be back."

"Hope you didn't have to shoot her to make her go," she said, and Earl shook his head with a quiet laugh.

"Told her I'd drag her out by the feet if she didn't take a break," he said.

"How long have I been in here?" she said.

"Since yesterday morning," he said. "You're in Springfield, by the way."

"If we're both here, who's minding the store?" she said.

"Don't sweat it," he said. "Staties and County are running patrols for us. And Bonnie is kicking ass. Got the whole shebang running like a Swiss watch."

"Good," she said. "That's good." She was lying on her side; she could feel bandages on her back. "How bad is it?"

"Doctor says you'll be fine," he said. "Minor scarring from the burns, so long as they can keep the infections away."

"Gavin?" she said. "Has anyone picked him up yet?"

"There's nothing to pick him up on, Dana," he said quietly. "He was a witness, like a couple hundred other people. We took his statement and let him go, just like all the others."

"Shelby said something," she said, struggling to think through the pain killers. "He said something. 'He doesn't want you.' Something like that. 'He doesn't want you. You didn't know.'"

"State bomb techs say they found pieces of propane tanks in the rubble," he said. "The big ones you run a grill on. Had to be twenty of them there. They went through his house this morning."

"The detonator was wireless," she said. "That takes some skill."

"They said the same thing. Trouble is, they didn't find anything there," he said. "No wiring, no timers or radio receivers. Not even a kid's remote control car. If he built that bomb there, he sure as hell cleaned up after himself. Didn't even find a pair of wire strippers or a soldering iron."

"Bet I know who built it," she said, and he nodded.

"For what it's worth, I don't necessarily disagree with you," he said. "I took his statement. Kid was a block of ice. You'd expect someone to be at least a little shaken up after seeing something like that, but he was calm as it gets. Hell, he looked bored."

"Not exactly grounds for a search warrant," she said, and he shook his head. "They shook hands, right before he went up to the bandstand. Possible Gavin slipped him the detonator."

"Possible," Earl said, nodding. "Fire is looking for it now. Say the kid's involved somehow. How's he convincing people to do it? Just telling them they should feel bad?"

"*Boszorkány*," Dana said. "That's what the old woman

called him. She said he makes people do what he wants them to do. Maybe he's some kind of psychic or something. Or, maybe I'm just stoned to the fucking gills."

"Now that's a distinct possibility," he said, laughing with her as the door opened. Macy stepped inside, carrying a tray of soft drinks and a bag from Hardees.

"Hey," she said, setting the food on the hospital tray and bending down carefully to give her a kiss. "You're awake."

"Hope so," Earl said. "Hate to think you're wasting a perfectly good dream on me." Macy laughed with them, sounding incredibly tired as she sat down on the edge of the bed. She slipped her hand into Dana's and gave it a squeeze.

"Well, I'd better get back," he said. "Someone's not there to keep those county idiots in line, and they'll have half the town locked up for littering or something similar."

"I should be back tomorrow," she said.

"We'll see about that," Macy said.

"Ain't no rush," he said. "Take care of yourself, let us take care of things at home for a bit." Earl left them alone, and when she saw the look on Macy's face, she knew she wasn't going anywhere today without one hell of an argument.

"Don't you even think it," Macy said. "I can see the wheels turning in there. You're actually about to try and walk out of here, aren't you?"

"I'll take it easy," she said. "Trust me, I'm in no condition to be working right now. But I can rest just as easily in my own bed."

"And from bed, it'll turn into 'I'm just going to check in with the guys'," she said. "After that comes 'I'm just going to catch up on some paperwork.' Next thing I know, you're right back at it. This is me you're talking to, remember?" She looked at her for a moment, and Dana did her best to look innocent.

"Damn it, Dana. You just got blown up yesterday. You don't have to be tough all the time, you know."

"I'm not," she said. "Look, truth is I hate hospitals. I'm supposed to rest, right? Well, I sleep best in my own bed, with the television remote in my hand and you next to me."

After the longest thirty seconds she could remember, Macy just shook her head. "I want your promise you'll stay in bed," she said. "No popping into the office, no checking up on anyone, nothing but Netflix and ice cream."

"Deal," Dana said. Macy shook her head and gave her another kiss.

"You really are one stubborn bitch, you know that?" she said, and Dana shrugged.

"It's all part of my charm," she said.

"I'll go let the nurses know," she said. "But you're on your own convincing the doctor."

"Fair enough," Dana said, settling into the bed as comfortably as her back would let her. She figured if she could talk her way past Macy, one doctor would be a breeze.

***

Three hours and one exhausting argument later, she let Macy help her into the passenger seat of her car, trying not to put too much pressure on her burns. She could feel wet spots in her shirt, and she knew some of the blisters were popping.

The doctor had sent her home with some decent painkillers, antibiotic pills large enough to choke Bigfoot, and an industrial-sized tube of ointment, along with a stern admonishment to see her doctor immediately if she showed any signs of infection or other side effects.

She slept most of the way back to town, waking up as Macy drove past the park. Yellow crime scene tape was everywhere, and she could see chunks of splintered wood everywhere. "Jesus," she said as she surveyed the damage. It was a wonder no one else had been seriously injured or killed.

"Could have been a lot worse," Macy said carefully. "You did that."

"Earl did that," she said, and Macy shook her head.

"Just take the compliment," she said, laughing. "You're a hard woman to worship, you know that?"

"Guess I'm not feeling so impressed with myself just

now," she said, staring at the damage as they drove away. "Don't know if you've noticed, but my batting average has sucked a little lately."

"Hey," Macy said, growing serious. "None of this is on you. You did the best you could. The best anyone could do, for that matter, and I'm willing to bet good old Earl would say the same."

She didn't know what to say to that, so she said nothing until a familiar face went past the window. Gavin was standing outside the hardware store, holding a brown paper bag and seemingly staring a hole in her. "Stop the car," she said.

"What? Don't tell me you want to stop by the office," she said. "You promised."

"Just stop the car, Macy," she said. Macy pulled over, and Dana got out, ignoring the pain in her back as she walked up to Gavin.

"Chief," he said. "Good to see you up and around. Didn't think they'd release you so soon."

"Wasn't as bad as it looked," she said. "How are you holding up? Can't have been easy seeing something like that, especially after what you've been through." The gambit was risky, but it paid off; she saw the barest crack in his carefully crafted facade. It lasted only a second, and when he looked up again he was smiling as if nothing was wrong, but she'd gotten through. "How's your great grandmother?" she said, hoping to keep him on his heels.

"Cantankerous as ever," he said with a grin. "Heard you had a little visit the other day."

"We did," she said. "Had a nice little chat. Care to guess what about?"

"Her favorite subject, no doubt," he said, the smile fading from his face. "I don't suppose I need to point out that she's not always lucid. I'm afraid the years are catching up to her faster these days. Poor thing gets confused so easily. Have to watch her like a hawk so she doesn't try to cook and burn the house down. Still, she's family, right? You do what you have to for family."

"I don't know," Dana said. "She seemed pretty sharp to

me.”

“That's the thing about dementia, Chief. It can be tricky,” he said. “So, what sort of colorful stories did she tell you? Maybe that I started the fire, or that I killed her cat. Well, that one's true, I'm afraid.”

“You killed her cat?” she said. “That something you do often?”

“Only when I don't realize they're hiding in the wheel well of my truck,” he said. “Felt just horrible about it, but I don't think she ever got over it. But you know what my personal favorite is? Honestly, I can't even get mad about it, because I get such a kick out of it. She has moments when she thinks I'm some sort of witch. At least, I think that's what the word translates to; I barely speak any Hungarian at all.”

“*Boszorkány*,” she said, and Gavin nodded, his melted face twisting into a chilling rictus.

“That's the one,” he said. “I'm sorry if she bothered you. Sometimes it's easier to just go along with her, you know?”

“I'm sure she's a handful,” she said, studying him for a moment. “You spoke with Mayor Shelby just before he died. Mind telling me what that was about?”

Gavin looked at her for a minute, and gave her another one of those terrifying smiles. “She got to you, didn't she?” he said after a minute. “She got you wondering about me. Maybe I used my witchy powers to make all those people kill themselves. That about right?”

“I think you know something about all this that you're not telling me,” she said as Macy walked up to them. “I'll find out what it is, Gavin. You can believe that.”

“Well, when you find out what it is, let me know,” he said, shaking his head. He stared at her for a moment, and she held his gaze. “Miss Macy, why don't you go wait by the car,” he said. “I'm afraid the Chief and I need to have a conversation.”

“She doesn't have to go anywhere,” Dana said, mostly to keep her from unloading on him. To her surprise, Macy had already turned and was walking toward the car.

“You did that to her, didn't you?” she said. “You did something to her.”

"Assume you're right," he said, crossing his arms. He leaned in for a minute and smiled. "Assume I can get inside someone's head, make them do whatever I want. Who's going to believe you?"

"Doesn't matter," she said. "It ends here, Gavin. No more killing. Walk away."

"Oh, has someone been killed?" he said. "I mean, I know some people committed suicide. Horrible as that is, I don't see how you can accuse anyone of anything."

"Fair warning, Gavin," she said. "Whatever this is, it's over. You got your revenge; let it go at that."

"Oh, I'm just getting started," he said, smiling. "Before I'm done, everyone who ever turned a blind eye to what those bastards did to me will pay." He pulled an old ball cap from his back pocket and put it on, nodding to her.

"Beautiful day," he said. "You should probably take it easy, Chief. Those burns of yours will take a while to heal if you don't take care of yourself. Trust me on this one." He took two steps backward before turning around and walking away, whistling as he strolled down the sidewalk to his truck.

"Son of a bitch," she said, standing there on the sidewalk and shaking. The sun was shining on her back, making it hot and more painful than it had been before.

She walked back to the car, where Macy was sitting patiently behind the wheel, staring straight ahead. She didn't move her head until Dana closed the door.

"Everything okay?" she said, starting the car.

"You tell me," she said. "You feeling okay?"

"Guess I didn't sleep very well last night," she said. "Maybe after we get you settled in, I'll take a quick nap."

"Probably a good idea," Dana said, wondering if she even suspected what had just happened.

CHAPTER TWENTY-FOUR

She lay on her side, watching Macy's slow, even breathing as she slept. She'd tried to get some sleep herself, but the burning ache in her back and her own mind wouldn't allow it.

Either she'd finally cracked, or Gavin was actually somehow making these people kill themselves. She remembered the look of terror on Shelby's face as he begged her to run. It was almost identical to the one Melody Hagerrman had worn as she struck the lighter. She'd been too far away to see, but she was willing to bet Henry MacNeil was wearing the same terrified look as he climbed out onto that ledge. That one hurt, mostly because of Mark.

"Shit," she said, looking at her phone. She'd lost track of a full day, and had almost missed his funeral. If she hurried, she could still catch the graveside service, assuming she bent the speed limit a little on the way into Springfield.

She dressed carefully, putting on an extra undershirt in case her burns seeped through. She was busy carefully trying to pull on her shoes when Macy sat up, still half-asleep and looking absolutely glorious.

"And where do you think you're going?" she said. "Wearing a uniform, no less."

"Dress uniform," she said, pointing to all the extra embroidery and the fancy Stetson on the dresser. "Mark's funeral."

"Baby, he'd understand," she said. "Hell, he'd probably be mad at you for coming."

"I wouldn't understand," she said. "He was my officer. I'm going."

"Then at least let me drive you," she said. She climbed out of bed and dressed quickly. "I'll even wait in the car."

"You don't have to do that," she said. "I don't mind being seen in public with you, you know."

"I know," she said. "But I'm not exactly dressed for a funeral, and we don't have time for me to fuss with it anyway. Just promise me you'll let me bring you straight home afterwards."

"Promise," she said. She didn't say it, but it had less to do with keeping Macy from worrying than it did not wanting to be out of town any more than necessary.

***

They made it to the cemetery with time to spare, thanks mostly to Macy's lead foot and her assurance no cop in existence would ticket her once he heard why they were driving so fast.

"The Sam Hill are you doing here?" Earl said as soon as he spotted her. "You're supposed to be in the hospital."

"I wasn't about to miss this," she said, ignoring the fact she almost had. "He was my responsibility." She spotted Travis and Wendall, also in dress uniform, standing near the open grave.

"County agreed to hold the fort for us," Earl said.

"Good," she said. She let him lead her over to Dr. and Mrs. Sherman. She shook hands with both of them.

"Chief, I understood you were in hospital and wouldn't

171

be attending," Dr. Sherman said.

"He wouldn't have let it stop him," she said. It was all she could say. Mark would have sucked it up to see her off; she owed him at least as much.

"Would you like to sit?" he asked, and she shook her head.

"No sir," she said. "I'll see him off properly." It was a true sentiment as far as it went, but she was also not entirely sure that if she sat down, she'd be able to get up again.

The pallbearers started bringing the casket down, and they lined up out near the head of the grave. They set the casket down gently on the straps that would lower it into the ground. Earl pressed something into her hand, and she thanked him as she placed his badge on the casket. She stepped back into line.

Ignoring the pain in her back and the worse pain in her heart, she stood up straight. "Ten hut!" she said loudly, and all of them stood at attention. She managed not to wince as she snapped a sharp salute, and the others followed suit. She held the salute despite the fact she could feel something trickling down the small of her back where more blisters had burst.

She stood at ease, and the men followed her example as the minister gave his final words. She managed not to cry mostly by focusing on the pain in her back; she'd cry later, in private. "Hold it together," an old lieutenant of hers had told her once. "No matter how much crap is coming at you, you hold it together. You don't break down in front of your men. You hold it together for them, and deal with it later, in private."

She held it together for the others, and by the time the service was over, she was only a little surprised to see they were all trembling, even Earl.

The crowd began to disperse, stopping to offer their condolences to the Shermans. She stood at the graveside as Earl stepped up to her.

"I liked the kid," he said. "Damn shame."

"Yes," she said, thinking of the gruesome smile Gavin had given her. "It is."

Earl looked over at her. "You know something," he said.

"It's Gavin," she said. "He's doing all this."

"You know this how?" Earl said.

"He admitted it," she said. "Practically dared me to do something about it. He killed MacNeil. That puts Mark squarely on his head."

"Then I say we take it out of his crispy ass," Earl said, and she nodded.

"Meet me at my house tonight," she said.

"I'll bring the beer," he said, nodding. "Should I let the others in on it?"

"No need," Travis said as they approached. "Look, we've been talking it over. I could maybe buy the first two incidents as teenage angst and copycats. Might even sell me on survivor's guilt for the staff. But what in God's name could Patrick Shelby have to do with any of it?"

"Seems like one huge suicide cluster," Wendall said, quietly. "Way outside the norm."

"Don't take a genius to figure out something's going on," Travis said. "Sounds to me like you two might know what that is. If it got Mark killed, we're in."

"My house, just after eleven," she said. "Should be nice and quiet."

"Bowling alley closes at ten," Wendall agreed. "Bar's outside city limits. I'm sure county won't mind if we let them play in their own sandbox for once."

"You are going to explain all this at some point, right?" Earl said, and she nodded.

"I'll tell you everything I know," she said. "But first I need to talk to someone."

They stopped to offer their condolences to the Shermans, and the others walked her to the car, where Macy was waiting. "Get in the car," she said as soon as she saw her face. Dana didn't argue; she just sat down gingerly. "You look like you're about to pass out."

"Wouldn't fight it at this point," she admitted.

"Go home and rest," Earl said. "We'll check in on you later."

She fished the bottle of pain meds out of her pocket and

swallowed one of them with a bottle of water Macy handed her. She wanted to sleep, but the pain was too bad. She settled for closing her eyes and trying to get comfortable as Macy started the drive back to town.

"I want to look at your back as soon as we get home," Macy said. "We'll probably have to clean you up and put on more ointment."

"Sounds like fun," Dana said, and Macy shook her head as she tried not to let her see the smile on her face.

"Are you really this tough, or just full of shit?" Macy said.

"Probably fifty-fifty at this point," Dana admitted as the painkillers started to kick in. She felt sleep tugging at her, and stopped fighting it.

***

She woke up when the car stopped, and it took her a moment to recognize her own house. "Look who's awake," Macy said as she turned off the engine.

"Sorry," she said, yawning. "Those pills must be stronger than I thought."

"Right, the pills," Macy said. "Probably has nothing to do with the fact you haven't been sleeping lately, right?"

"Who me?" she said around another yawn. "I sleep like a baby."

"Yeah, just like a little colicky baby," Macy said. "Sounded like you were having some pretty funky dreams."

"Not surprising," she said. She yawned again, and Macy shook her head.

"Okay, I'm calling it," she said. She got out of the car and walked around to the passenger side, opening the door and helping her stand. "You're going to bed, and I don't want to see you up for at least six hours."

"The guys are coming by at eleven," she said as they walked up to the front door. Macy fished the keys out of Dana's pocket, unlocking the door and letting them inside. She dropped the keys on the hallway table and closed the door, then practically dragged Dana up the stairs.

"I'll take this," she said, unbuckling Dana's duty belt and

setting it on the nightstand before pulling her shoes off. Dana started to lay down, but Macy stopped her.

"Nope," she said. "Not yet. Shirt off."

"I'm flattered," Dana said, "but I'm really not up for shenanigans right now." Macy smiled and shook her head.

"I need to get a look at those burns," she said, picking up the tube of ointment. "Judging by how wet that shirt is, I'd say you're seeping. Have to treat them before you get an infection."

"An infection," Dana said, nodding as she yawned again. She unbuttoned her shirt and slid out of it carefully. "Here comes the part that sucks," she said as she started to pull off her undershirts, wishing for once she was small-breasted enough to get away without a bra as she unhooked it.

"Let me help," Macy said, sitting down on the bed. Dana turned her back to her, and Macy pulled the shirt out and up, going slow to avoid rubbing her burns. She clucked her tongue. "Definitely need to change at least one of these dressings. Sit tight while I grab the stuff."

"You're the boss," Dana said with a smile.

"And don't you forget it, Chief," she said, grinning as she went into the bathroom. She came out a moment later with a bag of various bandages, gauze, and tape.

"You want me to use the adhesive remover?" she said, holding up a small bottle of clear liquid.

"That shit hurts worse than the tape," she said, shaking her head. Macy nodded and peeled up the corner of one bandage.

"Fast or slow?" she said.

"Fa—ow, shit," Dana said as Macy pulled the bandage off. "I knew you were going to do that."

"Sorry," she said. She applied the antibacterial ointment to the bandage and gently set it in place. "Well, the good news is that the last of the large blisters popped. Bad news is there's no good way to bandage it. It's going to hurt."

"Just promise me a cookie when it's done," Dana said as Macy set up the last bandage.

"You promise to keep your butt in this bed and give yourself time to heal, and I'll even throw in a chocolate shake," Macy said.

"Hard to argue with a tough negotiation like that," Dana said.

"Good," she said as she helped Dana slip on a nightshirt and lay down. "Now, you've got at least ten hours before the Stooges are dropping by for the big Scooby club meeting. I want you to sleep as much of that as you can, understand? It's not about being tough enough," she said as Dana started to protest. "You've proven that, time and again. Your body needs sleep to heal, Dana. Now, I have to go into the school for the big meeting that got rescheduled, but I'll be back in a couple of hours. And when I come upstairs, I expect to see your cute little butt fast asleep."

"Just my butt?" she said.

"Well, it is my favorite part," Macy said, giving her a careful kiss goodnight. "Now, remote's right here, you've got water on the nightstand, and I'll lock up tight."

"My gun," she said.

"You want it in reach?" she said, and Dana shook her head.

"I'm stoned off my ass," she said. "Lock it up. Safe in the downstairs hallway. Combination's your birthday."

"Wow," she said. "You're giving me the combination to your gun safe? Must be getting serious."

"Has been for a long time," Dana said, her eyes closing on their own. "You know that, right?"

"We'll talk when you're not tripping balls," Macy said, tucking in the blanket around her waist but leaving her upper body uncovered, just the way she liked. Macy picked up her duty belt and started trying to get the Glock out of her holster.

"I don't even know how this thing works," she said. "Doesn't that get in the way?"

"It's a retention holster," Dana said sleepily. "Push down and rock it forward."

Macy tried it three times before getting the gun out. "Tricky," she said, holding the gun carefully.

"Supposed to be," Dana said around a yawn. She was about to explain the benefits of a retention duty holster when she fell asleep.

She felt a light kiss on her temple, and smiled.

"Sweet dreams," Macy said, leaving her to them.

CHAPTER TWENTY-FIVE

"I'm coming, I'm coming," she called out as she climbed out of bed and made her way down the stairs slowly, aware of every injury as she walked to the front door. Whoever was there was apparently in a hurry to talk to her, because he leaned on the doorbell for a moment before going back to pounding on the door itself.

"Jesus, leave it on the hinges," she said, peeking through the curtains to see who the hell was beating her door down. Earl stood on the front porch, looking incredibly tired and old.

"Earl? What's the problem?" she said, still half asleep as she opened the door.

"Chief, I—I think you need to come with me," he said, sounding like he'd rather be anywhere else.

"Oh God," she said. "What's happened?"

"I think you should get dressed and come with me," he said.

"Come in," she said. He stepped inside and closed the

door as she went into the laundry room. She pulled a clean uniform out of the dryer and dressed carefully, trying not to pull anything open. Her shoes were upstairs, but thankfully she kept several pairs. She grabbed a pair out of the hallway closet and slipped them on without untying them to save herself bending over. She realized she had to go upstairs anyway; her badge was on her dirty shirt.

She left Earl standing in the living room and climbed the stairs, wincing at each step. By the time she made it to her room, she was starting to think Macy was onto something with the whole sleep and rest thing.

She bent down carefully and picked up the shirt off the floor, removing the badge and pinning it to her shirt before buckling her duty belt around her waist. She took a moment as she walked back downstairs for an honest assessment of herself, and decided she was okay to carry her weapon.

"Give me the rundown," she said to Earl as she opened the closet door. She punched in Macy's birthday into the safe panel, and the door clicked open. She froze as she reached inside, aware that something was wrong.

Like most cops, when it came to her equipment, she held firm to the belief that two was one, and one was none. Her spare flashlight, cuffs, extra cuff keys, canister of pepper spray, and folding knife were on the bottom shelf of the safe. The second shelf held her firearms; her extra duty Glock 17, and her backup, a Glock 26.

"Something wrong?" Earl said, and judging by the sound of his voice, he knew damned well there was.

"My duty gun's gone," she said. She pulled the extra Glock 17 out and loaded it, putting it in her holster. "Macy put it up for me when we got home so I wouldn't have to get out of bed. Maybe she couldn't get the safe open. I'll ask her where she put it tonight."

"Chief, I—I don't think that's going to be necessary," he said, and she had to do a double-take to make sure she was really seeing a tear run down his face. He wiped at it and stood up straight.

"Earl, I think you'd better tell me what's happening," she said, the first tinges of fear creeping up on her.

"It'd be best if you just come with me," he said, and she shook her head.

"Out with it, Earl," she said, by now well and truly scared. "Did—did she have an accident? She doesn't know anything about guns. What's happened?"

"Maybe you should sit down," he said.

"No," she said. "God damn it, Earl, what's going on? Where's Macy?"

He stumbled around it for a bit until he was able to get the words out. "An hour ago, we get a report of shots fired at the high school," he said, almost too quietly for her to hear. "I responded, half-expecting to find a bunch of kids setting off firecrackers in the Dumpsters or something. But when I get inside, I see—I found them in the conference room," he said.

"A shooting at the school?" she said, and he nodded. "Oh God, she was going to a meeting. Is she—is she okay?"

"No, ma'am," he said. "I'm afraid it's worse than that. It looks like—it looks like Miss Macy was the shooter."

"Bullshit," she said, letting go of the breath she hadn't known she was holding. "Jesus, Earl. That's not even funny. Is this why you dragged me out of bed?"

"Chief, please," he said. "I need you to hear me. I have half a dozen bodies on the ground. I have witnesses that got away when she started shooting."

Dana shook her head, closing her eyes for a moment and trying to keep it in check. It wasn't real, she decided. Just a drug-induced nightmare. There was no way it was real, not until she saw the body.

"Show me," she said after a minute. Earl nodded, holding the door open for her. She made herself walk out to the waiting patrol car, praying that for once Earl had made a rookie mistake and everything was fine.

✳✳✳

"Jesus," Dana said as she stood at the door to the conference room. Wendall and Travis were both taking photographs. The bodies hadn't been removed; they were waiting for county forensics. She was trying to keep herself calm and quiet as she studied the bodies, looking for one particular face.

"She's not here," Earl said behind her. "They took her to the hospital before I went to find you."

"She's alive?" Dana said, and he nodded.

"I'm sorry, Chief," Wendall said, looking like he was about to cry. "I heard shooting on my way past, stopped to check it out. I get here, and there's Macy, calmly shooting into the crowd. I ordered her to drop it, I swear to God. I must have said it a dozen times, but she just turned to me and raised the gun."

"Take it easy, son," Earl said as Wendall took several deep breaths. "You did what you had to do."

"Sounds like it to me," Dana said, patting the big man on the shoulder. "Whatever's going on, this wasn't your fault."

"Tell that to Macy," he said, getting back to work. Dana nodded as Earl looked at her.

"Go see your woman," he said. "We'll get this figured out."

***

Dana pulled into the hospital parking lot thirty minutes later and ran for the ER entrance. As soon as she asked for Macy, two security guards and a doctor came to see her.

"Where is she?" Dana said. "I need to see her."

"Chief, if you'll come with me, please," the doctor said.

"Just tell me," she said firmly. "And tell these two monkeys they can quit with the hard stare, I'm not impressed."

"Gentlemen, please," the doctor said, and the two security guards reluctantly left them alone. "I'm sorry about that, some sort of stupid hospital policy."

"Where is she?" Dana said. "I want to see her."

"I'm afraid there's no good way to say this," he said, and she backed away from him, shaking her head. She felt like covering her ears and screaming so she didn't have to hear what he was about to say next. Maybe if she didn't hear him say it, then it wouldn't be real.

"I'm afraid Miss Hester suffered several life-threatening injuries," he said. "Any one of them could have been fatal. Combined, there was simply nothing we could do. I'm afraid she passed away ten minutes ago."

She thought she might actually be okay for a minute; she thought she would be able to process it. She'd lost people before; her parents, friends. Even her little brother, who'd stupidly decided to ride his motorcycle home after drinking all night.

It wasn't until she realized that she was kneeling on the floor, and that the low, wailing sound she was hearing was coming from her that she understood what was really happening.

She managed to stand up and pull her shoulders back as the sobbing started to subside. "I'm sorry, what?" she said as the doctor said something she didn't catch.

"I asked if there was someone we should call for you," he said. "Did Miss Hester have any next of kin?"

"Um," she said, trying to cut through the fog enough to think. "Um, yeah. Her mother, a sister. I have their information somewhere. I'll take care of it."

"Chief, I understand you two were, close," he said. "We have several social workers on staff that can handle notifications."

"No," Dana said, shaking her head. "My town, my responsibility."

She pulled herself together long enough to drive over to Macy's house. She sat in the driveway for a moment, shaking as she tried to make herself get out of the car and go inside.

It was simple, she thought. Take it step by step. Step one, turn off the car. Step two, get out. Three, walk up the front steps and grab the spare key out from under the frigging hideous ceramic frog by the door. From there, it was just a matter of going inside.

Eventually she got out and made her way up the sidewalk, stopping to retrieve the spare key. Her hand froze in place as she went to insert it, but she made herself open the door. Macy had been just the sort of housekeeper Dana had never imagined being; she was sure she could go through the whole place with a white glove and not find a smudge of dust. She shook off the memories that were threatening to overwhelm her, and walked across the room to Macy's desk.

"Figures," she said, shaking her head at the neatly organized stacks of mail, the pencils freshly sharpened in an old coffee mug, and the general togetherness that was Macy. Had been, she reminded herself. Gotta keep it together, she thought.

She found Macy's address book in the middle drawer. Most people kept everything on their phones or computers, but Macy liked having things written down. "Batteries crap out at the worst possible time," she'd said. "And when you need to make the sort of calls you never want to, the last thing you want to do is look for a damned charger."

Sighing, Dana sat down at the desk, flipped the pages until she found the entry for her mother. She was about to dial when she stopped, and called her sister first instead. Macy's mother was well into her sixties, and not in the best of health. The absolute last thing she needed right now was to send a sweet little old lady into cardiac arrest over the phone.

The line rang three times, and she was waiting for voicemail to kick in when someone answered, out of breath.

"Turner residence, Linda speaking," she said.

"Linda Turner?" she said, verifying who she was speaking to out of habit. "This is Chief D—my name is Dana Atwater. I'm--"

"Macy's girlfriend," Linda said, her voice light and cheery. "Heard all about you. About time we got to talk. What's up?"

"I--" she started, her voice cracking as she tried to make herself say it. If she said it out loud, then it was true. "I don't know how to say it."

"What's going on?" Linda said, some of the brightness fading from her voice. "Is something wrong?"

"It's—it's Macy," Dana said, unable to stop herself from crying. "We—we don't know all the details yet, but--"

"Chief, what's happened to my sister?" Linda said, her

own voice shaking. "Is she hurt?"

"I'm afraid she's gone," Dana said, trying her damnedest to fall back into professional mode. "It seems there was a—a mass shooting at the school."

"Oh my God," Linda said, and Dana heard muffled sobbing.

"I need to stress, we don't know all the details yet," Dana said. "But it looks like—it looks like Macy was the shooter."

"Bullshit," Linda said, crying. "Macy wouldn't know a gun from her own ass."

"I know," Dana said softly. "But there were witnesses, survivors."

"Jesus Christ," Linda said, taking a deep breath that turned into a sob. "This isn't happening."

"I wish it wasn't," Dana said, her own voice flat.

"Shit," Linda said. "I have to tell Mom. Tell me you didn't--"

"I know she's in poor health," Dana said, shaking her head. "I didn't want to risk it."

"Thank you," Linda said. "I'm sorry, I need to--"

"No, I understand," Dana said. "If—when we learn anything new, I'll make sure you hear it from me and not the news."

"Thank you," Linda said quietly. "I'm sorry, I need to go. It's an hour drive to Mom's house from here."

"I'm so sorry," Dana said.

"It's just—where did she even get the gun?" Linda said. "She was up here last month, but it wasn't one of ours. She doesn't—didn't know anything about guns. Where'd she get it?"

"We're still looking into that," she said, closing her eyes and cursing herself for a damned coward. She wasn't ready to admit that part just yet, not to someone she'd never met.

Linda thanked her for calling and hung up, and Dana sat there at Macy's desk for a moment, feeling drained. She gave up and put her head on her arms, and started crying.

"Wow," someone said behind her. She stood and turned, her hand going to her weapon. "That looked like it was really hard to do." She drew and aimed as Gavin stepped out of the kitchen, his hands in the pockets of his jacket.

"Don't move," Dana said. "Show me your hands. Now."

"Which is it?" Gavin said, smiling. "Show you my hands, or don't move?" He took a step closer, and Dana raised the gun.

"Show me your hands!" she shouted. Her hands were shaking, but at this range she could hit him blindfolded. "Stay where you are and show me your fucking hands!"

Gavin stopped walking and pulled his hands out of his pockets, holding them up to show they were empty. "I think it's time we had a talk," he said.

"I should kill you right now," Dana said, her voice trembling.

"You probably should," he said, sitting down. "But you're not going to. Wanna know why?"

"I'll bite," she said, the gun still leveled at his heart.

"Because you want to know what I'm going to do next," he said, still smiling. "Because trust me, you haven't seen anything yet."

CHAPTER TWENTY-SIX

"Start talking," Dana said, not putting her gun away. "And I swear to God, if you even blink, you're dead."

"Well, we don't want that," Gavin said. "Well, I don't, anyway. I imagine right about now you've got a different opinion."

"Get to the point, or give me an excuse to shoot you," Dana said.

"You really should put that away," he said, smiling. "It'll make it much easier for us to talk."

"I'm good," she said, and he chuckled. She watched in horror as her hand moved on its own, holstering her weapon.

"Son of a b—how are you doing this?" she said as her legs carried her to the couch, and she sat down.

"It's complicated," he said. "Let's just stick to the basics. For instance, I could have just as easily made you put that Glock in your mouth and pull the trigger if I'd wanted to. You believe me?"

"I do," Dana said, shaking. "Why are you doing this?"

Gavin patted the arm of the chair and stood up. "Let me get you something to drink," he said. He went to the fridge and grabbed two of Macy's beers, opening them and setting one in front of her. "Do you know what it's like to be seen as some sort of useless freak?" he said. "Or maybe some sort of pitiful monster?"

"I know what it's like to be different in a small town," Dana said. "Can't say it ever made me kill people."

"Eh, I'm an over-achiever," he said with a shrug. His smile faded, and he stared at her. "I was a kid, Dana. I was a young, terrified kid who'd just lost his father, and almost died in the process. Do you have any idea what over thirty skin graft surgeries feels like? I do. You know what it's like to look in the mirror every morning and try to shave around this mess?"

"What happened to you was horrible," Dana said. "And it didn't have to happen. But you can't just kill them all."

"Can't I?" he said, grinning. The twisted scar tissue at the side of his mouth made it even more gruesome. "Seem to be doing a pretty good job of it so far."

"Gavin, you have to stop," she said. "You're killing innocent people."

"Innocent?" he said, laughing. "You're joking, right? You know what Chase and his asshole buddies did to me?"

"I do," she said. "If you'd come to me, I--"

"You would have done jack shit, just like everyone else," he said. "And you honestly think the sander was the worst of it? Trust me, it isn't even close."

"And what did Macy do to you?" Dana said, trying not to cry. "What was her crime?"

"She was part of the system," Gavin said. "Just like the rest of them. More worried about a winning season, willing to protect the important kids."

"Bullshit," Dana said. "She was the first in line to sign an affidavit saying the school covered it all up. She was in your corner, Gavin."

"Sure she was," he said. "Once it was already out in the open, and there was no risk. She ignored it just like everyone else."

"So what now?" Dana said, fighting to get control of her hand. She made her fingers twitch, and almost let out a yell.

"Well, we're working up to something, aren't we?" he said. "The big finish, if you will. Of course, what that will be is really up to you."

"Fine," she said. "Let go of my hands and hold real still, and it'll all go away."

"Nah," he said. "I'm having fun. Here's what's going to happen instead." He stood up and drained his beer. She was annoyed to find she was doing the same, and managed to put it down.

"Hmm," he said, nodding. "You must be strong. Most people can't even think about resisting when I turn it on."

"Just getting started," Dana said. Her hand started for her weapon, and he shook his head. Instead of pulling her Glock, she squeezed her boob instead.

"You can push back a little," he said. "I don't mind. Keeps it interesting. But I promise you, the next time you go for that gun, it's going under your chin."

"So what comes next?" she said, straining to move her arm at all and failing miserably.

"There aren't that many names left on my list," he said. "Honestly, I can forget about most of them. But there's one left that needs to pay, and you're in a wonderful position to help."

"I will never help you kill someone," she said. "You really might as well kill me now."

"Oh, I think you will," he said, smiling. "I could make you do it, but that wouldn't be as much fun. Besides, you haven't even heard who it is."

"I can guess," she said, and he laughed. "Earl Granby."

"He let the bastards get away with whatever they wanted, and they knew it," Gavin said, growing angry. "The others, I could almost understand. They were protecting the school, or at least that's what they told themselves. But Granby. He was the goddamn chief. He was supposed to enforce the law. Instead, he let them off the hook, time and time again."

"I won't hurt Earl," Dana said. "Hell, I doubt I could take him if I wanted to."

"You'll figure something out," he said. "Either Earl Granby dies, or I make one hell of a big splash."

"I'm going to stop you," she said. She growled in frustration as she actually unbuttoned her shirt.

"You think so?" he said, still giving her that horrible smile. "You have until tomorrow, or I get on with it myself. Nice tits," he added as he started for the door.

She stood there for several minutes, crying and shaking with rage until she could put her shirt back on, ignoring the pain in her back. She started to call Earl, but stopped. She definitely needed to talk to him, but not over the phone.

She had a feeling she knew exactly what Earl's answer would be, but she needed to hear it from him. She was just getting in the car when her phone rang.

"Atwater," she said, tired beyond belief.

"Chief, it's Bonnie. I have a lady here asking to speak to you."

"I'm a little tied up," she said. "Can she talk to Earl or one of the others?"

"Beg pardon, Chief, but she didn't come in to file a report," Bonnie said. "She says it's personal business, and she can only talk to you."

"Who is it?" Dana said. If it was that stupid reporter again, she was going to crap on someone.

"She says her name's Ilona, and she's very insistent that she can only talk to you," Bonnie said. "I can try to get her to make an appointment, if you'd like."

"No," she said, maybe a little too quickly. "Let her wait in my office, and keep her comfortable. I'm on my way in now."

"Yes, Ma'am," Bonnie said, and the call ended. She backed out of Macy's driveway just a little too quickly, and raced to the station.

She didn't understand exactly what was happening, but she knew Gavin was doing it, and the old woman would have answers. She at least hoped so, otherwise she didn't have a goddamn clue what to do next.

****

189

"You got a visitor," Earl said as she came into the office. "Otherwise I'd tell you to take your butt anywhere but here right now."

"Save it," she said. "Listen, I'm gonna see what the old girl has to say, and then we need to talk."

"I think you're probably right," he said, looking at the scared old woman sitting in front of her desk. "Let's go see what she has to say."

"I don't know if she'll talk to both of us," Dana said.

"Oh, Ilona and I go way back," he said. "And we even get along."

"Good," Dana said. "Because I just saw the weirdest goddamn thing I've ever seen, and I'm betting she can explain it."

"Your office," Earl said, and she led the way. Earl took the other seat in front of her desk, turning it around to face her.

"Ma'am," he said, and she smiled.

"Chief, I need to speak with you," she said, struggling with her English. "I think—I think he maybe do something very bad, very soon."

"I can't say as I disagree," Dana said.

"You believe, then," Ilona said, and Dana nodded. "He is *boszorkány*. He attack your mind."

"He sure as hell did something to me," Dana said, fighting not to shiver as she remembered practically undressing in front of him. "I was just at Macy's house. He showed up out of nowhere."

"He got the drop on you," Earl said. "You're not exactly at a hundred percent lately."

"That's just it," Dana said. "I never knew he was there until he spoke."

"Musta scared the hell out of you," Earl said, and she nodded.

"I drew down on him," she said. "He made me put the gun up. He thought it, I did it, no questions asked."

"He make people do what he want," Ilona said. "Give him money, whatever he want."

"He said he could have just as easily put the gun in my mouth instead of the holster," Dana said, nodding. "For what it's worth, I believed him. He wanted me to—he wanted me to kill you."

"Well, that figures. So, what's it gonna be?" Earl said. "Gonna poison my flask? Cut my brake lines?"

"Not funny, Earl," she said, and he shrugged.

"He's bluffing," Earl said. "I say we call him on it."

"Ilona, is there a limit to what he can do?" she asked. "Is there something too big for him?"

"No," she said, shaking her head. "Only limit is body. The magic, it take a terrible price from the body. Bigger magic, bigger price."

"I don't suppose he gave you any sort of idea about what this 'something big' will be?" Earl said, leaning against the wall and crossing his arms. "I can't imagine much bigger than what he's already done."

"It'd have to be huge," Dana admitted. She saw Ilona's face darken for a moment as she struggled with her English.

"You understand this? Bigger magic, bigger price. Maybe too big, body no last."

"Chief?" someone called out from the lobby. Sonya Anderson came in, frowning when she saw Ilona sitting in front of her desk. "Oh, Lord, what did you get up to now, Grandma?"

"Oh, we're just having a grand old time," Earl said with a smile. "Ilona here's got a million good jokes."

"Is she in any trouble?" Sonya asked, and Dana shook her head.

"As a matter of fact, no," Dana said. "She's just been helping us out a little. Local history."

"I not sure I clear. Sonya will put into English for me," Ilona said, standing up.

"Grandma, they really don't have time for--"

"Enough," Ilona said, slamming her cane into the floor and making them all jump. She rattled off a stream of Hungarian neither of them caught, but when she was finished, she sat back down, and Sonya looked properly chastised.

Ilona started talking, pausing for Sonya to translate. "My grandmother, she was *boszorkány*," she said. "It's an old word. Closest translation is probably witch."

Dana and Earl exchanged looks, and nodded. "What can they do? These *boszorkány*?" Earl asked, surprising them all with his perfect pronunciation. Sonya translated, and Ilona nodded before speaking again.

"You have to understand, she grew up hearing all this superstitious nonsense. It's practically a religion over there," Sonya said. Ilona barked something at her, and Dana half-expected her to whack the woman with her cane.

"She says they could do almost anything," Sonya said. "Read another's thoughts, control the weather, predict the future."

"Puppet master other people?" Dana said, and Sonya nodded as Ilona spoke again.

"She says her grandmother could control other people," Sonya said as Ilona continued. "She cured men of addictions, stopped husbands from straying. Good magic."

Ilona took her hand and said something quietly in Hungarian, and Sonya shook her head. "Grandma, no. Now that is enough. It's bad enough you filled his head with all this nonsense. I won't let you drag him into any more of it."

"No," Ilona said, tapping her cane again. "No more. I no be quiet any more. You know, Sonya. You know what he is, what he do. He is *boszorkány*. He good boy once, but he broken now. Now he do bad things. You know. You see."

"All I see is an old woman who needs to be in a residence facility," she said. "And that's happening first chance I get."

Ilona just smiled. "I not crazy. Judge even say so. You want me in hospital, so you get money. I not want it to be true, either. I love Gavin, same as you. But he do bad things now. Hurt others. Must be stopped."

"Chief, I'm sorry we've taken up so much of your time," Sonya said.

"Really, it's no trouble," Dana said. "She's welcome to come visit any time."

"Breaks up the routine," Earl said with a smile. "Ma'am,

might I help you to your car?" He held out an elbow, and Ilona let him guide her.

"You understand? Bigger magic, bigger price," Ilona said, and Dana nodded.

"I do," she said. "Thank you."

"He do something terrible, soon," Ilona said, and Sonya shook her head.

"Go on with the officer, Grandma," she said. "I'll be there in just a bit."

Earl escorted Ilona out, and Sonya shut the door. "I don't know what sort of nonsense she's been telling you about my son, but he's a good man," she said. "And I don't exactly need to tell you that the rantings of a senile old woman aren't grounds for an investigation."

"No, they aren't," Dana said. "But she doesn't strike me as at all senile. All that aside, I have a disturbingly large number of deaths in town, and all of them can tie back to Gavin. I wouldn't be doing my job if I didn't look at him."

"What you have is a large cluster of suicides, and one crazy teacher going postal," she said. Dana bit her tongue, but it still took a huge effort not to rip into her. "I think the next time you want to speak to my son, you should do it through our lawyer. And in the future, if my grandmother wanders in here alone, I expect a call. Am I clear?"

"Until a judge rules her mentally incompetent, your grandmother is a free woman, who can come and go as she pleases," Dana said. "And since you seem to like to throw around threats, I'll add in that if I find out she's being restrained or held against her will, you can be damned sure I'll arrest anyone and everyone who had a hand in it. Am I being clear?"

She gave Dana the barest nod, and walked out. Earl came in a moment later, and closed the door.

"You heard what she was saying, right?" Earl said, and Dana nodded.

"I did," she said. "And I think I have an idea how to use it."

CHAPTER TWENTY-SEVEN

Dana stood at the door to the station, watching the people milling around the square and drinking coffee that was quickly turning her stomach into a churning nightmare. Earl was helping Bonnie find a particular form in the nightmare that was his filing system, and Wendall was out on patrol.

"Like I said, it's pretty much a nightmare," Earl said. "Feel free to set it up however makes sense to you, and don't be afraid to ask for help. Ain't no sense in you lugging boxes I put up wrong."

"I'll get it squared away," Bonnie said. Earl gave her a grin and left her to it, pouring his own cup of coffee and joining her at the door.

"Is it just me, or is it awfully busy out there for a Wednesday morning?" he said, and she grunted. "You'd think no one was open for business."

"Not many are," she said. "Hardware store, barber shop, the fabric store, even the dollar store are all closed down."

"Some kind of holiday I forgot about?" he asked, and she shook her head.

"You always were a cock-eyed optimist, Earl," she said. "Notice no one seems to be really headed anywhere? It's like someone threw a party, and they're all just hanging out."

The park wasn't just busy; there were throngs of people milling about, laughing and joking with each other. She saw the few teachers who'd escaped Macy's shooting spree, along with the school board and the city council, all chatting happily next to what had been the bandstand. The debris had been cleared away, but the concrete pad still showed singe marks from the explosion. The radio crackled, drawing her out of her contemplation.

"Chief, it's Wendall," he said over the radio. "I hate to jinx the whole thing, but it's dead out here. Like too quiet."

"Come on in," she said. "Looks like there's some sort of gathering at the park."

"Copy that," he said, and the radio went dead. His patrol car pulled into the designated spot in front of the station a moment later, and he headed straight for the coffee pot as he came inside.

"Look who's here," Earl said, pointing toward the bandstand. There, standing at the edge of the concrete, was Gavin Anderson, dressed in a suit that was probably a couple thousand dollars outside his means. Then again, she figured if he could make people commit suicide or go on a shooting spree, convincing them to fork over a little cash was no big deal. "You know what he looks like to me?"

"Someone dressed for a special occasion," Wendall said. They both looked back at him, and he just shrugged. "Please, anyone with half a brain knows he's up to something. I don't know exactly how or what, but he's a bad guy."

"You're not wrong," Earl said.

"Would I believe it if I asked?" he said, and Dana shrugged.

"Maybe, but you might sleep better if you didn't," she said.

"You know what I'm not seeing?" Wendall said. "Look

at how many folks we got out here. Most of the town, right?
You got knuckleheads that could start a fight in a nunnery,
chumming it up with the deputy mayor and the city council.
Dyed-in-the-wool assholes chatting with little old ladies, and
everyone's smiling."

"Regular Rainbow Coalition, ain't it?" Earl said.

"A what?" Wendall said, and Dana shook her head,
smiling. "Point is, we're looking at what should be an all
hands on deck situation. Should at least have to be working
the crowds hard to squash the stupid before it starts, right?
So how is it I get the feeling we could sit down and play
cribbage without a care in the world?"

Dana was trying to find the best way to answer when the
entire crowd, some hundred people, all stopped what they
were doing and turned to them. It might have been just her
growing paranoia, but she could swear every single one of
them was staring directly at her.

"Yeah, 'cause that's not creepy at all," Wendall said.

"Pretty sure our deadline just came and went," Earl said
quietly. "Think maybe we should go join the party?"

Dana nodded. "Wendall, grab a rifle," she said. He
looked surprised, but did as he was told. She went to her
desk and grabbed her backup, a Smith and Wesson model 36.
She double-checked the cylinder before snapping it closed
and handing it to Bonnie, butt first.

"You familiar with this?" she said, and Bonnie nodded.

"Got one just like it on my nightstand," she said.

"Good," she said as Wendall came back with one of the
AR-15s on a single-point sling. "Once we step outside, you
lock the door behind us, and don't open it for anyone."

"Not even you?" she said, and Dana shook her head.

"We've got keys," she said. "Someone forces their way
through the door, you don't hesitate. Can you do that?"

"Yes, Ma'am," she said, nodding. "What's going on,
Chief?"

"I'm not sure," she said, checking her own weapon. "But
something tells me it's about to get very hairy, very fast.
Earl, you know what to do?"

"Shit," Earl said with a grin. "Been wanting to do this

since the whole nonsense started. Hell yes, I'm ready."

"Good," she said.

"Chief, mind filling me in?" Wendall said. "Why do I get the feeling we're about to get into one hell of a fight?"

"Just stay loose," she said. "If and when I give the signal, you take down Anderson. Understand?"

"Not really," he said, chambering a round. "But I'm good to go."

"Okay then," Earl said, checking the chamber of his .45 and reholstering it. "Let's go pick a fight."

***

Gavin was sweating despite the cool morning air; it was taking more effort to control the crowd than he'd thought it would. His stomach was beginning to cramp, and he had one hell of a headache brewing, but it didn't matter. It would all be over soon.

He focused, ignoring the headache as he made the crowd go quiet and turn to face the Chief's office. She'd been standing there in the doorway, just watching, for over an hour. If he didn't know better, he'd say she was hiding.

He hadn't really expected her to kill Granby, of course; that had mostly been a way to screw with her, to show her what she was dealing with. It didn't matter; he had a plan for the old man either way.

He was about to actually call her out, just to get on with it, when the door to the station opened, and she came strolling out, with the old man and the big cop behind her.

"Showtime," he whispered with a grin, unaware of the small trickle of blood coming from his nose as he maneuvered the crowd into position.

***

"Heads up," Dana said as they stepped into the street. The crowd split into two, leaving an open lane through the crowd up to Gavin, who was smiling. Dana saw the blood

197

dripping down his face, and what Ilona said suddenly made sense. "Bigger magic, bigger price," she said, and Earl nodded.

"Maybe we'll get lucky and he'll blow a gasket," he said.

"When are we ever lucky?" Wendall said. "And is he really controlling all these people? What is he, some sort of psychic?"

"Close enough," Dana said. "We live through this, and I'll fill you in."

"I'm gonna hold you to that," he said as they stopped at the edge of the crowd. He jumped back, raising his rifle as the crowd moved in unison, producing an array of pistols and large kitchen knives.

"Chief?" he said, but Earl just put his hand on the rifle and lowered it.

"The kid's the only one that matters," Earl said, and Wendall nodded.

"Just so you know, I'm taking a fucking boatload on faith here," he said, and Dana nodded.

"No time like the present," Earl said, and Dana nodded. He stepped forward, squaring his shoulders and hooking his thumbs into his gun belt. Had any of the townspeople been in their right minds, they'd recognize it as his "ready to whip some ass" stance.

"Gavin Anderson," he called out, his voice booming in the quiet morning air. "Heard you got a bone to pick with me."

"I surely do," Gavin said, stepping forward. He stopped a few feet from them, and Dana found her hand moving to her gun on instinct. "Chief, if you clear leather, everyone here will be dead before you get a shot off." Just to prove his point, the entire crowd pointed their weapons at themselves; guns went to temples, and blades poised over hearts, the tips actually piercing clothing.

"Well, I ain't exactly hard to find," Earl said. "But instead of bringing your beef to me, you do this. Way I see it, that makes you just about the biggest chickenshit sumbitch I ever saw, and I've seen a lot."

"You think so?" Gavin said. "With a thought I could

make you give that fancy little gun a blowjob."

"But you ain't," Earl said. "Fact of the matter is, you're hiding behind a whole lot of folk that don't have shit-all to do with any of this. Know what I think? I think you ain't got the juice to take on a real man. Sure, you can get a bunch of snot-nosed kids to hang themselves. Make that damned fool mayor blow himself to Kingdom Come. Even make a sweet lady like Macy shoot a bunch of folks like fish in a barrel."

"I can do so much more than that," Gavin said. "Officer Wendall, kindly turn that rifle on the good Chief." Dana watched as Wendall, his face shaking with effort, aimed the rifle right at her head. More blood began gushing from Gavin's nose, and small bloody tears appeared at the corner of his eyes.

"You ain't looking so hot, son," Earl said. "Might oughtta call it a day before you have a stroke."

"You're gonna pay," Gavin said, shaking and sweating as blood stained the front of his shirt. "You'll all pay."

"Well, here I am, you little shit. Come and take what you want, if you can," Earl said, unsnapping his holster.

"No," Dana said as her hand moved on its own, pulling her Glock and aiming it at Wendall. "No, damn it."

"Chief, you do what you gotta," Wendall said, shaking. "I don't know how long I can fight whatever this is. Drop me before I do it."

"No," Dana said, her hand shaking. She was still shaking with effort when the shot rang out.

Wendall fell to the ground, clutching a bullet wound I his right arm. Dana turned to see Travis wave to her from the rooftop, and she gave him the thumbs-up.

"You good?" she asked Wendall, who nodded as he groaned.

"Shit, no," he said, laughing. "Fucking asshole shot me."

"Not bad," Gavin said, smiling. Blood continued to flow over the scars on his face, making him appear almost demonic. "Chief, if Earl isn't dead in the next thirty seconds, everyone here dies."

"What's the matter, son?" Earl said. "Too much of a

chickenshit pussy to do it yourself? Come on, take your shot."

"Earl," Dana said, grunting as she tried to fight it, but her gun was moving toward him just the same.

"Yeah, I thought so," Earl said. "Still the same little candy-ass whining shit you've always been. What, your balls get barbecued along with the rest of you? That's it, isn't it? You're pretty much junkless now, aren't you?"

Dozens of pistols cocked at once. "Shut up, old man, or you're gonna get all these people killed."

"Bullshit," Earl said. "You're gonna kill them, not me. How about you be a man and own what you're doing for once, instead of crying about everything? Jesus, no wonder those kids shit on you so much. It wasn't because you're some crispy critter freak. It's because you're a little bitch."

"Shut up," Gavin said, shaking harder as blood flowed from his ears and nose.

"Shut me up," Earl said, holding his arms out wide. "Take your best shot, kid. I beat your old man's ass more times than I can count, but at least he had the balls to do the fighting himself."

Gavin's control was slipping; Dana was able to put her gun down, and she saw several people in the crowd looking confused as they lowered their weapons.

Gavin reached out and grabbed a knife from a confused-looking housewife, shoving her aside. "That's it," Earl said, smiling. "Come on, boy. All that killing, about time you got your hands dirty. Come on." Earl held his hands up, ready for a fight.

Gavin started forward, but stopped, his hands going to his head as he dropped to his knees and screamed. Earl backed off, looking confused as the crowd moved away.

"Enough," Ilona said, leaning on her granddaughter's arm with one hand and pointing at Gavin with the other. She muttered something Dana couldn't hear, and Gavin screamed louder as blood began spurting from his eyes.

She wasn't surprised to see the old woman was crying as she walked forward, led by her sobbing granddaughter. "No more," Ilona said, crying. "No more, Gavin. Is over. No let you hurt anyone. Not ever again."

"Grandma," Sonya said, crying, and Ilona looked up at her. Gavin stopped screaming, and collapsed on the ground. Dana took the opportunity and landed on him, cuffing his hands behind his back as he lay unconscious.

"Must be done," Ilona said. "You see what he do."

"He's my son," Sonya said. "There has to be something we can do, some other way. We don't have to kill him."

"I will need books," she said. "From my trunk."

"Earl, take her to get whatever she needs," Dana said, hauling Gavin to his feet. Her back screamed at her as the wounds reopened, but she ignored it.

"You know what to do?" Ilona asked, and Sonya nodded.

"I haven't forgotten what I was taught," she said, wiping her cheeks. "Just please, help him."

"Come with me, Ma'am," Earl said. "We'll get you there and back in a jiffy."

"What is jiffy?" Ilona asked, and Earl smiled.

"For what it's worth," he said as he helped her into Wendall's cruiser, "I didn't want to kill him."

"But you would," she said, and he nodded.

"In a heartbeat," he said, and she patted his hand.

"Good," she said. "If this no work, may be necessary."

"You said you know something about all this?" Dana asked as they carried Gavin into the station. She had an awkward moment as she fished out her keys, but she managed to get him into a chair, cuffing him to it.

"There are ways to keep him asleep," Sonya said, sniffling. "Some herbs to burn, some chanting. I have everything in my purse. I'll just go get it."

"Better hurry," she said as Gavin groaned. "Bonnie, Wendall's outside with a gunshot wound he's pretending is no big deal. Do me a favor and kick his ass to the hospital, will you?"

"If I have to, I'll call Mom," she said, nodding as she grabbed her keys.

CHAPTER TWENTY-EIGHT

"I thought you didn't believe in any of this stuff," Dana said as Sonya placed a small brass bowl on the floor near Gavin's cot. She lit a small bed of wood shavings in the bowl, then added a pungent mix of herbs from a leather pouch.

"I don't practice the old ways," she said, wafting the smoke over Gavin's unconscious body. She placed a small wreath on his chest, then chanted something in a foreign language Dana just assumed was Hungarian. She didn't really need to know what it was; she just needed it to work. She was already exhausted from fighting Gavin's influence, and she didn't know if she had another round in her.

"You seem to have it down," Dana said. "Although, for all I know, you just summoned an other-worldly pizza."

"My mother was a devout practitioner," she said. "I grew up in it. Now I'm a Baptist. Still, just because I don't practice it doesn't mean I've forgotten, or that it doesn't work."

"You knew what he was doing, all this time, didn't you?" Dana said, fighting not to get angry.

"I didn't want to know," she said quietly, standing up and backing out of the cell. "Who wants to believe their child is a monster?"

"But if you suspected he could do these things, why wouldn't you try to stop him?" Dana asked. "Why did so many people have to die before you got involved? Why did--"

"Why did it have to be her?" Sonya said quietly, and Dana nodded. "I don't have an answer for you. But even if I'd known, I'm not *boszorkány*. I don't have the gifts, not like my grandmother or Gavin. I'm not a witch."

"You could have come to me," Dana said.

"And said what? Help, my son is a revenge-crazed psychic monster? I'm sure that would have gone over well."

Dana shook her head. "We could go around and around on this, and never get anywhere," she said finally. "I don't blame you."

"You blame him," she said, and Dana nodded.

"All those people," she said, her voice catching. "Macy. As far as I'm concerned, that's all on him."

"He did what he did," she said, nodding. "But he was pushed to it. Surely you can see that much."

"What I see is a kid who got dealt a truly shitty hand in life," Dana said. "But instead of doing something with it, he decided to kill a lot of people. He made a choice to do that, and he needs to pay for it."

"Look at him," Sonya said, pointing to the scars twisting his face. "Hasn't he paid enough?"

"Not by half," Dana said.

"He's sick, Chief," she said. "Assuming you could even begin to prove any of this, no court would hesitate to declare him insane."

She went back into the cell, adding more herbs to the burning bowl. "Why not just tranq him?" Dana said.

"Because lucid dreaming is like child's play for a *boszorkány*," she said. "The herbs will suppress his abilities, at least for a while. Hopefully long enough for grandma to get back.”

“And what is it she's going to do?” Dana said. “Will it be permanent?”

“Best guess? She's going to bind him so he can't hurt anyone any more,” she said. “I don't know. This is next-level magic we're talking about. Well above my pay grade.”

“I get this is hard for you,” Dana said, trying to keep her voice soft. “I won't pretend to understand how hard.”

“My son was lost to me a long time ago,” she said, sniffling. “I just want to get back whatever is left of him.”

“I need you to hear me,” Dana said. “If whatever Ilona is going to do works, and he's neutralized, great. I'll probably spend the rest of my life trying not to put a bullet in his head, but I'll deal. Believe it or not, but that's what I'm hoping for.”

“And if not?” she said, crying softly as she held Gavin's hand.

“Then one way or another, I'll stop him. I won't let him hurt anyone else,” Dana said, and she nodded.

“You're talking about murder,” she said.

“I'm talking about survival,” Dana said. “But yeah. If it comes down to it, I'll do what I have to do and deal with the consequences.”

✳✳✳

“So, does any of this have a chance in hell of actually working?” Earl said as he drove Ilona back to the station. The old woman had gone quiet since they'd left the house with the stack of books sitting in the back seat.

“Hard to say,” she said. “Is up to Gavin. He want to stop, it work. He no want to stop, it no work.”

Earl nodded. “So, what are we going to do?” he asked. “Like an exorcism, or something?”

“Is old magic,” she said. “My *nagymama* teach me, many years ago. If work, it take away his power.”

“And if it doesn't?” Earl said. “I don't mean to sound cruel, ma'am, but that boy is responsible for a lot of deaths. Some of them mattered a lot to me.”

204

"Is my fault," she said, wiping away a tear. "Foolish old woman, hope he not become bad after all bad happen to him. Should have done long ago."

"Ain't your fault," Earl said. "Now, I ain't saying that boy ain't been down every backroad in Hell, but he did what he did on his own. He chose to do those things, you understand?"

"I sorry for your friends," she said. "The boy, the teacher. I like her."

"So did I," Earl said. He pulled the cruiser into one of the designated spots and killed the engine. "Ma'am, I gotta ask. If this, whatever the hell it is, doesn't work, are you gonna get in my way?"

"No," she said with a sad shake of her head. "If no work, then Gavin lost for good. Better he die than continue to do bad."

"And his mama?" he said. "Can't imagine she's gonna stand by and do nothing."

"How you say? We cross that bridge when come to it?" she said, and he nodded.

"Guess there's no point in putting it off," he said. He got out and went around to the passenger side, opening the door and helping her out.

"I make it," she said. "You get books. Careful with books, very old." Earl just tipped his hat and let her start for the door, then collected the stack of books from the back seat. He didn't have a problem believing most of them were older than all of them put together, and probably worth more than his own hide.

Sonya opened the front door as Ilona approached, and held it open as Earl carried the books inside. "Lord, what is that smell?" he said as he set the books down on the counter.

"Sage, white thistle, opium, a few other things," Sonya said, and Earl raised an eyebrow.

"Opium?" he said, and Dana shrugged.

"At this point, does it really matter?" she said, and Earl just shrugged.

"Hell, if it puts an end to this crazy shit, we can open a meth lab in the storage locker," he said. "Not like we couldn't use the help with the budget. Where's the girl?"

"Sent her to take Wendall to the hospital," Dana said. "Figured the less people in on this, the better. Travis is on patrol."

"So, long as he doesn't arrest anyone, we're good," Earl said, and she laughed.

"He's on duty on his day off," she said. "They'd have to be chucking severed heads out the window for him to even do a traffic stop."

Ilona went into the cell with Sonya, who helped her kneel down on the floor in front of the brass bowl. "More sage," the old woman said, and Sonya added it to the bowl.

"I need that book," Sonya said, pointing. "The big red one."

"Got it," Earl said, picking it up and bringing it to her. Gavin was stirring, groaning and putting a hand to his head as Earl stepped back.

"Best get a move on," he said as Sonya opened the book in front of Ilona.

"Mom?" he said, sitting up. The wreath fell off his chest, and he stretched. "What's going—Grandma? Are you trying to do what I think you are?"

"It's okay, Gavin," Sonya said. "It's for your own good, son. You have to stop."

"But why? It's so much fun," he said, grinning. He squinted at her, looking frustrated as she continued to help Ilona. "Why isn't it working?"

"Be over soon, boy," Ilona said. She picked up the wreath and crumbled it in her hands, adding it to the increasingly putrid fire in the brass bowl on the floor.

"No!" he said, standing up and trying to kick the bowl. He must have been dizzy, because he fell over instead, landing on the cot as Ilona began chanting in Hungarian.

"Just relax, Gavin," Sonya said. "It's okay, son. It's all going to be okay. Don't fight us, son. Just lie down and relax."

"I can help with that," Earl said. Before anyone could think to stop him, he walked into the cell and hit Gavin square on the chin, knocking him out cold.

"Hey," Sonya said as Earl rubbed his knuckles and walked out of the cell.

"He had that coming," Earl said.

"We must hurry," Ilona said. "I need *kés*. How you say?" She made a sawing motion with her hand.

"A knife," Sonya said. "She needs a knife."

Dana pulled her Spyderco out of her pocket and flicked the blade open, handing it to her. The old woman took a deep breath, then drew the blade across her palm with a hiss.

"Jesus," Dana said as she put the knife down and held her hand over the bowl, letting the blood drip into the fire. She waved her hand in front of her face as the smell hit.

"Oh, good Lord," Earl said. "Why does that smell like you're burning a cat's ass?"

"Shh," Ilona said, and they shut up. Sonya handed her a bone, and she stirred the whole mess together. "Is time. If you pray, now good time."

"Not sure the Lord would much approve of this one," Earl said. "Then again, He sort of left it up to us this time anyway." Dana just shook her head at him, and he shut up again.

Sonya opened Gavin's shirt, revealing the mass of scar tissue that covered his chest and abdomen. "Chief, now might be a good time to lock that cell door," she said. "This could get bad."

"How bad are we talking?" Dana said, closing the door.

"Bad enough I don't want him getting out of this cell," she said. "If it works, he might get violent."

"And if it doesn't?" Dana said.

"Then we both dead," Ilona said. She started chanting in a quiet voice as she dipped her fingers in the nasty concoction before tracing a design on his chest. She sang what sounded like a hymn as she painted his skin, the deep ridges of scar tissue breaking up the lines she drew.

She traced a cross on his forehead, and stood up straight, her face pained from stiff joints. "Is done," she said, sounding incredibly tired.

"That's it?" Earl said. "I don't know what I was expecting, but I guess I figured there'd be something more to it."

All four of them jumped as Gavin screamed, his back arching as he thrashed around on the cot. Dana started to unlock the door, but Ilona shook her head.

"No," she said. "Door stay locked until over."

"Chief," Earl said, sounding like he'd just been slugged in the face. "You seeing what I am?"

Dana took a good look at Gavin, and she saw it; steam rising from the goo Ilona had painted on his chest. She heard the unmistakable sound of skin sizzling, and Gavin screamed louder as the mixture burned into his skin.

She was about to unlock the door anyway just to stop it when bright white light erupted from his chest, making it almost impossible to see. She shielded her eyes in time to avoid the worst of the light, but she was still seeing spots when the light died out.

Gavin had mercifully stopped screaming, and was unconscious. Sonya covered him with the thin blanket, and kissed his forehead. "I'm sorry, baby," she said. "There was no choice. I hope you'll understand that some day."

"Is he—is he dead?" Earl asked, and Ilona shook her head.

"No," she said. "He live. He may want different when wake, but he live."

"Good," Dana said. "Will he remember all of this?"

"Every moment," Sonya said, wiping her face.

"Good," Earl said. "He should have to live with it."

"We just stripped away a huge part of who he is," Sonya said. "It's not unlike losing an arm. I'd say he's suffered enough."

"We'll agree to disagree there, ma'am," Earl said, and Dana shook her head.

"Is it over?" she said, and Ilona nodded.

"Is over," she said. "I must rest now. Very big magic, very big price."

"What do we do with him?" Earl said, pointing to the cell where Gavin was sound asleep.

"I'd suggest a suicide watch," Sonya said.

"We'll put him on a ninety-six hour hold, if you'll sign the papers," Dana said, and she nodded.

"I think that would be best," she said, still crying. "I'm sorry about your girlfriend, and your officer, and all the others."

"Thank you," Dana said. She watched as Sonya led Ilona out of the station.

"It's not enough," Earl said, shaking his head. "He kills God knows how many people. Granny gives him a little owie, and it's all better now? Not good enough by half."

She pulled her Glock and held it out to him, butt first. "Go ahead if you think it'll help," she said with a shrug. "Won't bring any of them back."

Earl looked at the gun for a moment, then shook his head. "If he was coming at me, sure. But I got enough blood on my damned hands as it is. Don't need any more, especially not some kid sleeping in a locked cell."

"Then it'll have to be enough," she said, putting her gun away. "At least it's over."

"Almost," he said, and she raised an eyebrow. "You get to explain all this happy crap to Travis and Wendall."

"Lucky me," she said.

CHAPTER TWENTY-NINE

Six Months Later

Dana pulled up to the Anderson house and got out of the car, adjusting her duty belt as she climbed the stairs. Sonya was waiting for her on the front porch. "How is she?" she asked, and Sonya shook her head.

"It won't be long now," she said. "Doc Tremblay's in with her now. Down the hall, second door on the right."

She stepped inside, still fighting the reaction to reach for her gun when she saw Gavin staring at the television. "Chief," he said, casually and politely enough, but still with a boatload of awkward tension. She supposed it would never really go away, on either end.

"Gavin," she said. "How are you holding up?"

"Honestly, I don't know," he said. "I love the old gal, but she's suffering. Maybe it's for the best if she goes quick."

"Sometimes that's best," she said, still fighting the urge to shoot him. When he gave her a sad smile, the scar tissue still distorted, but there was no malice in it this time.

"She's awake, if you want to see her," he said, and Dana nodded. She went down the hall, knocking quietly on the partially open door. Doc Tremblay answered, looking tired as he let her in.

"Chief," he said. "You can visit, but keep it brief. She doesn't have long."

"I won't be long at all," Dana said, nodding.

"So silly," Ilona said from her bed. Dana got a good look at her, and was shocked. She looked so much smaller, so frail compared to the last time she'd seen the old woman, and it sank in that she was really dying.

"What's so silly?" Dana said, sitting on the side of her bed and taking her hand.

"So much fuss over old woman," she said with a tired laugh. "I dying. Sleep not help." She looked at the doctor, and Dana nodded.

"Doc, think you could give us a moment?" she said, and he nodded.

"I could use some air," he admitted. "You holler if anything changes."

"He mean if I die while he not here," Ilona said with a grin. "I think he scared he miss it."

"I been tinkering under your hood since I got out of med school," Doc said with a tired smile. "Ain't about to miss this."

He left them alone as Dana smiled. "Should be babies," Ilona said, looking around. "Old woman should die with many fat babies nearby."

"Maybe next time around," Dana said, surprised at how sad she was.

"No look so sad," Ilona said, patting her hand. "I tired. Is time. But need tell you something first."

"Should I go get Sonya to translate, make it a little easier?" Dana said, and Ilona shook her head.

"No," she said. "This part she no hear. This just for you, and for handsome old man." She smiled, and Dana laughed. Earl always did have a way with the ladies.

"I'm listening," Dana said.

"Gavin better now," she said. "No more *boszorkány*. No more hurt."

"I can tell," she said. "I can see how guilty he feels."

"Nothing last forever," Ilona said, and Dana nodded.

"He'll get through it," Dana said. "I guess we all will."

"No," Ilona said, coughing. It turned into a violent coughing fit, and Dana handed her a handkerchief. When it stopped, there was blood in the middle of it. "Nothing last forever. Not even old magic."

"What are you saying?" Dana said, suddenly terrified she knew exactly what the old girl meant.

"Old magic tied to *boszorkány*," she said. "I die, it die. Not happen fast, but will happen."

"Are you saying he'll get his powers back?" Dana asked.

"And probably the crazy with it," someone said behind her. She turned to see Gavin standing in the doorway, his arms crossed.

"I sorry," Ilona said, crying. "I try."

"It's okay, Grandma," Gavin said, looking sad. "You did your best. Not your fault." He crossed the room and bent down, kissing her cheek. "You should rest."

"I tired," she agreed, closing her eyes. "Thank you for coming to see old woman, Chief."

"Of course," Dana said. On impulse, she bent down and kissed her cheek as well.

"Chief, I think we should talk," he said, and Dana nodded. "Not here. I don't want Mom to hear this."

"Come by the station later," she said, looking back at Ilona, who'd gone back to sleep. She waited until she saw her chest rising and falling slowly. "After."

"Count on it," he said. "And Chief?"

"If you're about to try and apologize, don't," she said, fighting to control herself. "There's nothing you can say."

"I guess not," he said.

✳✳✳

"Highway Patrol just sent this over, Chief," Bonnie said, handing her a fax. "I'm sure they'll make it official later, but

212

I bugged them to get it to me sooner."

"Thanks," Dana said. "I swear, this place has never run better."

"I heard that," Earl said from under his hat. His feet were up on the desk, and she'd have sworn he was asleep.

"You telling me I'm wrong?" Dana said, and he chuckled.

"Not even close," he said as she looked over the fax. "Well, you gonna keep us all in suspense?"

She read it again, just to be sure. The state police had ruled she had no culpability in Macy's action; she'd been under the influence of prescribed narcotics at the time, and Macy had taken advantage of her situation to steal her weapon. It was a tidy crock of shit, but it would have to do.

"Well, Staties won't be arresting me any time soon," she said, dropping the fax on her desk.

"Figured that much," Earl said. "I know you ain't gonna believe a damned word of what I'm about to say, but it wasn't your fault."

"I know," she admitted. It was the first time she'd missed the opportunity to blame herself. "Doesn't make it any better."

"Nothing much will," Earl said. The phone rang, and Bonnie picked it up on the first ring, just like always. Had to give it to the girl, Dana thought. She's really on the ball.

"I understand," Bonnie said. "Yes, I'll pass it along. Thank you for calling." She ended the call and stood up, walking back to Dana's desk. Given the fact their desks were only a few feet apart, Dana guessed it had to be bad news.

"That was Doc Tremblay," Bonnie said. "She passed away twenty minutes ago."

"Thank you," Dana said as Earl nodded.

"Rest in peace, old gal," he said quietly. The bell above the door, one of Bonnie's improvements, rang as the door struck it, and Gavin Anderson stepped inside.

"Bonnie, you mind running down to the store and grabbing us some doughnuts?" Earl said, handing her a bill from his pocket. "I don't eat a doughnut every couple of hours, I forget I'm a cop."

"Sure," Bonnie said. "Chief, you want anything?"

"Just Earl's metabolism," she said, and they both laughed. Bonnie grabbed her jacket and headed out as they both approached the front counter.

"Chief," Gavin said. "Detective."

"Gavin," she said, and Earl just gave him a nod and a suspicious look.

"Guess we should have that discussion now," he said, and Dana nodded.

"Come on back to the interview room," she said.

"Be right there," he said as he and Earl eyed each other.

"Behave, both of you," she said, leaving them alone as she headed back to the interview room. She turned to look back, and just shook her head as the two shook hands. She knew Earl well enough to know there was one hell of a threat behind that handshake, and judging by the look on Gavin's face, he got the message loud and clear.

Wendall came in from the back door, looking annoyed as he headed to his computer. His shift was supposed to have been over an hour ago.

"Mind watching the front for a couple minutes?" Earl said, looking back at the interview room door where Dana stood with Gavin. "Bonnie'll be back in a moment."

"Sure," he said, eyeing Gavin with every bit as much suspicion as Earl had. "Everything good?"

"Not so much, but when is it ever?" Earl said, and Wendall nodded as he walked away.

***

"I won't try to apologize," Gavin said, "because like you said, there's nothing I can say that would help. I won't try to explain it, either, because honestly I doubt it would make much sense."

"So what then?" Dana said. "If none of that, why are we here?"

"I think you know why," Gavin said. "You heard her, just as clearly as I did."

"Heard what?" Earl said.

"Ilona," Dana said. "Before she died, she said the magic

214

was tied to the person performing it. When she died, I guess it died."

"Meaning my gifts are already coming back," Gavin said. "I can feel it. And not just my gifts; all of it. I guess when she took them away, she took some of the psychosis with it."

"Hold on," Earl said. "Are you saying we're gonna have to do this whole happy horse-shit dance again?"

"No," Gavin said. "You know, I remember all of it. Every damned thing I did. Every minute of it, and it's killing me. I'm already a freak. I don't want to—no, I won't be a monster again."

"Then don't," Dana said. "Make the choice to let it go."

"I can't," he said. "That's what I'm telling you. I take the pills, every day. Like clockwork, I choke them down, and I see my therapist, and none of it is helping."

"You're saying--" Dana said, and he nodded.

"Either you can do it, or he can, or I can do it myself," he said. "But someone has to stop me, and now."

"You're saying you want one of us to kill you," Earl said.

"I'm saying I won't go back to what I was," he said. "I'll do it myself if I have to, but I'm scared. If you're worried about the legal consequences, I can make damned sure you have a good reason to shoot me."

Dana was quiet for a moment. "You know, damn near all I've dreamed about for the last six months is putting a bullet in your skull," she said. "Thought of a hundred different ways to do it, and get away with it. Maybe ten would have worked."

"And now?" Gavin said. "Here I am, right in front of you, asking you to do the very thing you want to do so bad your palms are itching."

"And I can't just shoot a man in cold blood," Dana said. "Macy wouldn't want that, and I won't let you destroy what's left of her memory for me."

"Fair enough," Gavin said. He looked over at Earl. "You're a more practical sort, aren't you? You know what's going to happen if I start again."

"Be lying if I said the idea of shit-kicking you from here to St. Louis and back don't put a grin on my face," Earl said.

"I killed plenty of men in my time. Guess one more ain't gonna send me anywhere I ain't already headed."

"Earl," Dana said, and he shook his head.

"Ma'am, you and I both know he's right," Earl said. "Last time he got a head full of steam, we were ankle deep in bodies. I don't think I can take the chance."

"What about the binding ritual?" Dana said. "We could try that again."

"There's no one to do it," Gavin said. "I can't do it to myself, and it's not like there's a magic shop on the corner by the Kum-n-Go. I need someone to do this. Can you do it?"

"For what it's worth, you seem like a decent fella with your eggs in the right basket," Earl said. "But if it means avoiding all that mess again, yeah. Ain't saying I won't lose some sleep over it, but I can do it."

"I can't be a part of this," Dana said, starting to leave.

"Chief, you need to see it happen," Gavin said. "In a moment, I'm going to attempt to disarm the good detective here, giving him no choice but to shoot me in self defense. It will go a lot easier on him all around if there's a witness," Gavin said.

"Ain't no skin off my back either way," Earl said. "Wouldn't be my first questionable shoot. Young Gavin came in under the pretense of giving us a statement about something he saw happen a few months ago. Turns out it was a ruse to get one of us alone, jump us for our gun. I was just a little faster, that's all."

"Sounds good to me," Gavin said. "Everyone knows you could beat the balls off a brass bull."

"Exactly," Dana said with a sigh. "Even with all the boneheads in this town, no one is stupid enough to take Earl on. It'd look suspicious, like suicide by cop."

"Good point," Gavin said. "Maybe I should go for your gun instead."

Before she knew it was coming, Gavin had her pinned to the wall and was trying to get her Glock out of her retention holster. Earl grabbed him by the shirt and tossed him backwards as he got the gun out and raised it.

"Put it down!" Earl shouted as he drew his own weapon,

and fired. The bullet caught Gavin in the heart, and he fell backward, already dead as he slid down the wall. Dana stood there in shock as Wendall came crashing through the door, his gun drawn.

"What the holy fuck?" he said.

"He got my gun," Dana said, looking suitably shaken, mostly because she was.

"Didn't give me a choice," Earl said, covering him as he kicked Dana's Glock out of the way. Wendall bent down and checked his pulse, then shook his head.

"What the hell was that all about?" he said. Dana, not sure she trusted herself to admit it, just shook her head.

"His great-grandmother just passed away," Earl said. "They were close."

"Well, shit," Wendall said. "I don't suppose if I asked somewhere off the record, there's a snowball's chance either of you would tell me what really happened?"

"Best you don't know, son," Earl said. He handed over his weapon. "Now, best get on with it. Chief, I take it I'm on administrative leave for the time being?"

"I'm sorry, but yeah," Dana said. "You know the drill."

"Shouldn't be too much trouble," Wendall said. "All on camera, right?"

"I wish," Dana said, thankful she'd remembered to turn the damned thing off on the way in. "We hadn't gotten there yet. He just said—said he needed to give a statement about what happened. At the school."

"Right," Wendall said. "Look, you don't want to tell me, I don't have to lie if I'm asked. But I'm not an idiot."

"I know that," Dana said. "Trust me, it's better this way."

"Well," he said, looking around. "I walked in and saw your Glock in his hand, so his prints will be on it. Earl only fired one shot, and I heard him clearly order him to drop the gun first. Up to the DA, but it all says good shoot to me."

"Better go ahead and give them a call, then," Earl said. "I'll just go grab a seat and cool my heels."

Bonnie came in the front door as they all piled out of the interview room. "What did I miss?" she said when she saw their faces.

"Trust me, sis," Wendall said. "You didn't miss out on a damned thing."

"Better call the coroner," Earl said, jolting them all out of their shock-induced stupor.

"I'm on it," Wendall said, securing Earl's .45 in his desk drawer and picking up the phone.

"I just have one burning question," Earl said, and they all looked at him. "Miss Bonnie, did they have any crullers?"

EPILOGUE

Dana stood in front of the grave, trying not to cry. "God, I hate coming out here. I never know what to say," she said, looking down at Macy's stone. "Everyone all agrees I'm not supposed to blame myself, you know. I didn't know you'd--"

She stopped, kneeling down and touching the stone. "I wish I could make it different," she said. "At least make everyone know why. What really happened. But I can't even give you that, babe. So much I never gave you."

She brushed away a splash of mud. "I'm so goddamn sorry, Macy. I just—it hurts. It hurts more than I can take some days."

She stood up and kissed her fingertips, then touched the M in her name. "I love you," she said, and walked three rows over to another, fresher grave. It would be months before Gavin's stone was erected; instead, there was a simple metal post with his name and dates.

"I want to hate you," she said. "You took everything. You practically destroyed this town. You took away the one person in this whole shitty world who meant anything to me, and you destroyed her memory in the process."

She felt a savage but brief urge to kick over the temporary marker, but kept it in check. She was about to leave when she heard footsteps behind her, and turned quickly.

"You're not the only one who lost everything," Sonya said as she approached. "Not saying one is any worse than the other, mind you. Just that we both lost everyone we loved."

"You lost them," Dana said. "Macy was taken from me."

"And you killed him for it," she said. "Oh, don't look so damned shocked. Like I believed that bullshit story about him taking your gun? I know, okay?"

"I don't know what you think you know," Dana said carefully.

"I know he asked you to do it," she said. "He asked me first, believe it or not. But I couldn't do it. What mother could? But when he had a chance, when he could think clearly enough to make a choice, he chose to die rather than hurt anyone else. That says a lot about who he was, don't you think?"

"I can't forgive him," Dana said, and Sonya shook her head.

"No one expects you to," she said. "And I'm not saying he was blameless. All I'm saying is, maybe make room for the possibility that he was a victim in all this, too. But hey, if it makes you feel better, you won, Chief."

"No one won," Dana said, shaking her head as she walked away.

Families all over town were grieving, the school was effectively shut down until further notice, and she'd buried the woman she loved. It was a sad, shitty end to the whole affair, but it was the bitter truth.

Sometimes, being a survivor just meant being left alone to try and pick up the pieces.

THE END

ABOUT THE AUTHOR

Some say he was born from unauthorized genetic testing. Others say he was found alone in the wilderness as a baby and adopted by a Special Forces team as their mascot. Still others say he was born smoking a pipe, although how he managed to keep it lit is still a topic of great debate.

Whatever his origins, Michael Chambers now lives in and works in Seymour, MO. When he's not writing or plotting world domination in a complicated scheme involving demonic mind control and sentient toasters, he enjoys shooting, martial arts, and flying RC helicopters.